SAINT THOMAS AQUINAS
AND THE PREACHING BEGGARS

Saint Thomas Aquinas
AND THE PREACHING BEGGARS

Written by Brendan Larnen, O.P., and Milton Lomask

ILLUSTRATED BY LEONARD EVERETT FISHER

IGNATIUS PRESS   SAN FRANCISCO

Cover art by Christopher J. Pelicano
Cover design by Riz Boncan Marsella

Published in 2005 by Ignatius Press, San Francisco
ISBN 978–1–58617–038–7
Library of Congress control number 2004109130
Printed at Brilliant Printers Pvt. Ltd, Bangalore, India; D0887, November 2016

CONTENTS

I

THE JOUSTING LESSON

S EATED ON a gray war horse, Thomas let his eyes roam over the big field in front of the castle of Rocca Secca in south central Italy. Some distance away, near the castle gates, he could see some of the serving men— varlets they were called—sunning themselves in the tall grass. Behind the varlets, sitting sidesaddle on their riding horses, were his mother and one of her maids. He waved his lance in the air, and his mother replied with a flutter of her white handkerchief.

Then he saw the exercise-master cantering toward him on a white horse. The handsome animal pawed the earth as it was brought to an abrupt stop.

The exercise-master was the oldest of the knights of Rocca Secca. His bony face wore the scars of a dozen sword fights. His green eyes glistened in the warm sun of an early spring morning in the year 1239.

"All right, Master Thomas", he said. "We'll try it once more before we call it a day. Do you think you can do it right this time?"

"I'll try, Sir Knight."

"Try hard." The old knight rose in his stirrups and glared at Thomas. "Let me remind you that you are not learning another childish game now. You are learning how to joust. Jousting is a man's business. It is one of the noblest arts of war and knighthood." He glanced toward the two women sitting so erect on their riding horses near the castle gates. "Try hard, Master Thomas", he repeated. "It would do your mother's heart good to see you do it right just once. Is your armor comfortable enough?"

"It will do", Thomas replied.

As a matter of fact, the long coat of mail he was wearing was painfully uncomfortable. Unfortunately, no better could be found. Most of the knights of Rocca

Secca were away, fighting for the emperor. Few coats of mail remained in the castle storehouse. In a long search a few days before, the varlets had found only one that would fit Thomas. It did not fit him well. It was tight, for, at fourteen, Thomas was big for his age—chunky like his father. He had his father's broad shoulders and barrel chest.

"All right, now", the exercise-master said, reseating himself in his saddle. "I'll direct you from the usual spot."

He rode off, stopping in the center of the field.

Thomas made himself ready. He let go of his horse's reins. In jousting, the rider's hands are busy with his equipment. He has to guide his mount with his knees. Following the exercise-master's instructions, Thomas ran his left forearm through the inner loops of his shield. His right hand took a firmer grip on his lance, a shaft of stout ashwood, ten feet long.

"Crouch!" The exercise-master's first order came hurtling down the wind.

Thomas crouched. He bent low over the horse's mane. He adjusted his lance, holding it level with his right hip.

"Charge!"

He dug in with his spurs. As the big war horse shuddered into action, Thomas kept his eyes on a dummy hanging from the crossarm of a post at the far end of the field. Stuffed with straw, the dummy had the shape of a headless man. Fastened to its breast was a shield like the one on Thomas' forearm. In the fretful April wind, the headless figure dangling from the crossarm twisted this way and that.

Thomas knew what he was supposed to do. No matter which way the dummy twisted, his job was to handle his lance so that its steel tip struck the dummy's shield squarely in the middle. If he succeeded, he would know at once. There would be a loud, clanging sound. If he failed . . .

Psssst!

As the giant war horse shot past the dummy, nothing came to his ears but the hiss of passing air. He had failed. He had failed again! His lance had not so much as nicked the edge of the dummy's shield!

Thomas wanted to cry. Not that he himself cared whether he ever learned to joust or not. He wanted to cry because his mother was watching. Far to the rear he could hear the exercise-master's scratchy voice.

"Recover!" the exercise-master shouted.

Obediently, with a backward thrust of his knees, Thomas brought the powerful horse to a halt. Under his tight armor his body was fearfully hot now. He could feel the sweat running in rivers down his face. Shifting his lance to the other hand, he lifted the visor of his helmet. He picked up the reins, turning his horse in the direction of the castle.

The varlets were still sunning themselves in the tall grass, but the womenfolk—his mother and her maid— were leaving the field. He watched as their light horses bore them across the drawbridge and the huge castle gates were drawn back to let them in. He checked an impulse to hurry after them, to beg his mother to stay and watch him while he tried just once more. He knew why she was leaving; she was leaving because five times he had tried to strike the shield on the dummy. Five times he had missed, and she was disgusted with him!

The exercise-master had joined him. The old knight reined in his mount so that the two of them sat face to face.

"Master Thomas," he said sternly, "when was the first time you ever practiced jousting?"

"Well, Sir Knight, it was the last time I was home from school."

"How long ago was that?"

"I don't exactly remember. It was shortly before Father and my brothers went away to join the army of the emperor."

"Six months, eh?"

Thomas nodded. "About that, Sir Knight."

"And who trained you?"

"My brothers."

"Sir Landulph and Sir Ronald, eh? How long did you practice out here under their guidance?"

"About ten days."

"Ten days!" The old knight's green eyes shot heavenward. "Holy Mother of God and all the saints!" he muttered. "Meaning no blasphemy, Master Thomas, but I am beginning to think that you are hopeless, that never, never will you become a knight. Let me speak to you forthrightly. I do not have to tell you that there are no better lance men anywhere than your brothers. As for your father, the Lord of Aquino . . ."

The old man's voice lifted. Respect and pride seized him at the thought of Thomas' father.

"Here in Italy, Master Thomas," he went on, "in Sicily, in France, in Germany—indeed throughout the length and breadth of the Holy Roman Empire—your father's fame as a jouster is justly known. I trained him myself, and I tell you that on the very third day of his training he struck the shield on the practice dummy square in the middle. But you, Master Thomas—you are hopeless, hopeless!"

The old knight gave the reins of his mount a tug so that the fine animal reared in the air. "Hopeless!" he shouted. "I give you up. I give you up!" With that the aging knight put the spurs to his horse. The animal flew across the field with him, across the drawbridge, and through the still-open castle gates.

A long, low sigh flowed out of Thomas. The tears he had been fighting tumbled from his eyes and down his broad, brownish cheeks. He saw the varlets getting to their feet and ambling into the castle. He saw the castle gates slowly close behind them.

He felt shut out and alone—more alone than he had ever felt in all his fourteen years. He remembered what the monks at his school had told him—that a person was never alone because there was always God. But for the moment God, too, seemed far away.

He looked about. The wind was livelier now. It raced through the grass, making a moaning sound here and there. And the sky, he noticed as he looked up, was a clean, flat blue, empty of clouds.

He sighed again and, with a flick of the reins, headed his big war horse in the direction of the castle gates.

2

THE LADY THEODORA

Like many of the castles built in the Middle Ages, the era of the knights and the crusades, Rocca Secca was enormous. Its battlements enclosed many acres. Fully two hundred people lived within them when all the knights were home.

It stood on a flinty hill. It was this hill that gave the castle its name, for in the Italian language *Rocca Secca* means "Dry Rock". On three sides the castle walls stood straight up from the hillsides. They were thirty feet high and at least a third as thick, and the seven towers were even higher and thicker. The largest of them, the great donjon tower at the rear, soared some seventy feet into the sky. Day and night a lonely peasant stood watch on its outer platform. The black and yellow banner of the Aquino family fluttered from its conical roof.

Thomas guided his war horse slowly across the field toward the castle gates. Reaching the drawbridge, he halted. Far below he could see a varlet crawling along the rocks fringing the moat. The varlet was a big man, looking twice as broad as he actually was in his dirt-colored shirt and baggy woolen trousers.

He was a familiar figure to Thomas. The sight of him lifted the boy's spirits. He leaned from his horse as far as his heavy armor allowed.

"Yo, ho, Fellow!" he called. "Looking for frogs down there?"

Fellow looked up with a start. The movement was too sudden. His bare feet lost their grip on the slippery rocks and he tumbled, with a splash, into the scummy waters of the moat.

Thomas roared with laughter. "I hope you can swim", he shouted.

"Good saints alive!" Whatever else Fellow had to say was lost in the hollow beating of his arms against the water.

Two strokes sped him to shore. He wriggled across the rocks on his stomach. He got to his feet and climbed the bank—a husky man with a rough, solemn face and a dark mustache drooping like a tattered curtain from his upper lip.

"What's got into you, Master Thomas!" he scolded with a scowl. "You shouldn't have scared me like that. It was a big one that got away. Me and my brothers—we could have made a meal out of that frog."

Fellow was Thomas' personal varlet. When Thomas was home from school, Fellow slept in front of his bedroom door at night. It was Fellow who took him back and forth to school.

The young varlet came quickly up the bank, slapping the water out of his clothes. He halted suddenly, staring at the boy and tugging at his damp mustache.

"Master Thomas!" he exclaimed. "What's the matter with you? What's gone wrong?"

"Nothing. Nothing at all."

"Come now. You're not a boy to tell fibs. There's something else you're not the boy to do. I never saw you weep but once in your life. That was when you were three years old and your baby sister, God rest her soul, was killed by lightning in the storm. You ain't wept since, Master Thomas—not until this day, that is. Come now! What's behind those tears you've been shedding?"

"Nothing." Thomas bristled. His mother had told him never to complain in the presence of a servant. It was wrong, too, for a person of noble birth to confide in a servant. But when he looked into Fellow's rough, solemn face, and when he remembered that there was no one else around to whom he could spill his troubles, he burst into tears afresh.

"Didn't you see what happened?" he wailed. "Out there on the lists—out on the jousting tournament grounds, I mean?"

"I didn't see but I can guess. There's no love of war and killing in you, Master Thomas, and those who are trying to put it into you are making a mistake—your mother among them, begging your lordship's pardon." Fellow had come alongside the war horse. He dropped his hand on the boy's foot in the stirrup. "Come", he said. "We'll go into the castle. I'll get you out of that steel they've buried you in. Then we'll have a talk about it. What do you say?"

For the time being Thomas was too choked up to say anything. He could only nod.

Turrets flanked the castle gates—two jutting towers, each with its high steel grill. As they reached the end of the drawbridge, the scrawny face of an old porter appeared in one of the barred openings.

"Open up!" Fellow shouted at him.

The porter made a face. "On whose orders?" he demanded.

"On my orders, old skin and bones. Be quick about it now. This is Master Thomas I have here."

"How do I know it's Master Thomas with all that armor around him? How do I know it isn't the wicked emperor come to grab some more of our knights for his army?"

"Oh, shut up and open the gates."

The porter was laughing. He had snarled at Fellow for the fun of it. He had already given orders to open the gates. His was a boring job, sitting behind the grill all day letting people in and out of the castle. It gave him a little pleasure, now and then, to swap insults with the other varlets.

Thomas was frowning as his horse carried him through the opening gates. "Fellow," he said, "why do all the varlets hate the Emperor Frederick?"

"Who says they do?"

"You heard the porter. He called him 'wicked'."

"Isn't the emperor a relative of yours, Master Thomas?"

"Why, yes. He's my cousin."

"Then I'd better not say anything bad about him."

"Please, Fellow. I won't be angry. Is the emperor wicked?"

Fellow's eyes lifted in a sharp glance at his master. "Is the devil?" he inquired.

"Fellow! What a thing to say!"

"You asked, Master Thomas. You asked."

They were in the main court of the castle now, an area known as the bailey. It was an enormous place, crowded with buildings separated by narrow alleys, most of them damp and sunless. Hugging the castle walls on their left were the stone barracks where the knights lived. There was a chapel with its stained-glass windows, a carpenter's shop, the smithy where the knights' armor was made and kept in repair, and the cookery shed where the castle meals were prepared in mammoth ovens.

There were people everywhere: peasants from the village at the foot of the hill, newly arrived that morning with carts full of grain to be placed in the castle store-house; varlets going about their duties; old knights loafing near the fountain while their squires, the youths who attended them, squatted on the pavement nearby, playing at backgammon or chatting of sword fights and jousting tournaments.

Thomas and Fellow went at once to the stables. There Fellow and a groom lowered the boy from his high horse. Fellow unloosed the straps of the boy's helmet and removed it, after which the groom pulled the fifty-five-pound coat of mail up over Thomas' head. Underneath he was wearing a black habit, the garment worn by the students of his school at the Benedictine Abbey of Monte Cassino, not far from Rocca Secca.

"There, now, Master Thomas," Fellow said, "you can breathe again. Shall we be on our way?"

They threaded a number of dark alleys. Their destination was the palace, the residence of the Aquino family, standing in the shadow of the donjon tower. At the far end of the bailey, cutting the castle in two, was a high, thick wall with its own moat, drawbridge, and gate. Beyond this lay the inner court, the front yard of the palace.

It was a pleasant place, paved with flagstones and cooled by a fountain in a grove of poplar trees. Above the arched entrance to the palace was a multi-colored mosaic of the Blessed Mother of God. As Thomas and Fellow entered, the boy breathed a Hail Mary; he always did. They crossed the great hall, a cave of a room filled with shadows under its vaulted roof, and went up a stone stairway that curved with the palace wall.

Thomas' room was long and narrow, with pointed windows at the front end. It was furnished with stone benches and wooden chairs.

Thomas flung himself on the bed, and Fellow removed his boots. After that, the husky varlet seated himself on one of the benches and gazed solemnly at his master. "All right, now," he said, "what's your trouble?"

Thomas sighed. "That's my trouble." He was pointing at the table in the middle of the room. It was a big table cluttered with books and paper.

Fellow turned and looked. "Your books, Master Thomas?"

The boy nodded. "I like to read and write. If I had my way, I wouldn't do anything but read and write and think all day long." He slipped from the bed and sat down on the bench next to Fellow. "Is it wrong?" he inquired.

"Is what wrong, Master Thomas?"

"Wanting to read and write and think all the time."

Fellow considered the matter for a second, tugging at his mustache. "Well, now, Master Thomas," he said finally, "you're talking to a man who can't read or write or think. I hear tell, however, that the ability is a gift from God. So what can be the harm of it?"

"It could be harmful, Fellow. A person could read and write and think the wrong things."

"I know that, Master Thomas. But surely the good Benedictine monks are teaching you the right ones."

"Indeed they are. And what you say is exactly what Brother Bell Ringer says."

"Brother Bell Ringer?"

Thomas chuckled. "'Bell Ringer' isn't his name. We call him that because that's what he does. He's an old monk at the abbey. He can't read or write himself, but he says those who can should thank God for the privilege. He says they should thank God every minute of the day and make the most of it."

Fellow was inclining his head vigorously. "Your Brother Bell Ringer", he said, "sounds like a man of good sense. There now. That problem's settled, isn't it?"

"No. It isn't settled because there's Mother." Thomas looked at Fellow, and Fellow matched his look with one of equal understanding. "Mother", the boy continued, "says it's all right for me to read and write and think while I'm at the monastery with the monks. But when I'm at home, she says, I should spend all my time learning the arts of war and knighthood."

Thomas would have spoken on, but the hall door had opened. Fellow muttered, "Speak of the devil!" and sprang to his feet.

It was Thomas' mother, Lady Theodora. In her youth the countess had been perhaps the most beautiful woman in Italy, and much of her beauty lingered on. Her eyes were large and dark in a cream white face. There was only a hint of gray in her blue-black hair, which fell in long braids on her shoulders.

People who knew Lady Theodora well spoke of her as having a man's mind and a man's will. She was a proud woman. The fact showed itself in every move of her slender figure. Theodora could never forget that she was the daughter of the Count of Teano and that she had married an even more powerful noble, the Lord of Aquino. She could never forget that she and her husband were related by blood to practically every crowned head in Europe, including Frederick the Second himself, the emperor of the Holy Roman Empire.

Not that any of these things prevented her from being soft and charming when it suited her purpose. She could be as soft as any woman, and more charming than most. She was at her most charming as she stepped into the room, saying in a low voice, "I would like to speak to my son alone, Fellow."

"Yes, my lady."

Fellow was out of the room in the time it took him to give his mistress a bow and close the hall door behind him.

Lady Theodora seated herself in the arm chair nearest Thomas. It was a huge chair. It swallowed her up. Unhappy as he was, Thomas was amused. A laugh bubbled to his lips.

His mother gave him the full force of her dark eyes. "What is so funny?"

"You!"

"I?"

"I don't mean you yourself, Mother. I mean you in that chair. I've always thought of you as a big woman. Now I realize you're really very tiny."

Theodora withdrew her eyes and smiled. She was beautifully dressed in a full-length, fur-trimmed gown with trailing sleeves and an over-tunic of pale green silk. "You have a sense of humor, Thomas", she said. "It's not a bad quality, provided you don't let it get between you and important things. One of your uncles had a sense of humor, and it cost him his head. He had the bad taste to laugh at a king when the king fell off his horse into a mud puddle."

Thomas had to laugh. So did his mother. Suddenly, however, she was serious again. "Oh, Thomas, Thomas," she said in an anxious voice, "why do you have to be so different from your brothers? What in the world is going to become of you?"

He ran to her at that, dropping to his knees and placing his big head in her lap. His voice came to her, muffled by the silken folds of her garments. "I'm sorry about this morning, Mother."

"And I am heartbroken. Every time you charged the dummy, I thought to myself, surely he'll strike the shield this time. Every time you failed."

"I tried."

"Did you?"

The sharpness of his mother's question brought Thomas' head up with a jerk. He looked at her, puzzled.

"Don't you believe me?" he asked. "Don't you think I was really trying?"

Theodora shook her head. "I'm sure you wanted to please me. Perhaps you even thought you were doing the best you could. The fact remains, you were not. I'm certain you could learn jousting in no time if you really wanted to. I'm equally certain that you don't want to."

"But, Mother . . ."

Theodora lifted her hand, causing the long trail of her sleeve to shiver. "I have not finished, Thomas", she said. "As I was about to say, I am sending you back to your school at the Abbey of Monte Cassino."

"At once?" Thomas tried to sound matter-of-fact, to hide from his mother his pleasure at this turn of events. "But I thought I was to remain home another week."

"What's the use? I brought you home so that you could learn jousting. Now the exercise-master tells me it is no use. You won't learn; you simply won't. You might just as well be in school as wasting your time here."

Lady Theodora had risen. She lifted her voice: "Fellow, will you come in again, please?"

The door opened immediately, and Fellow entered, dipping his head in respect. "Tell me," she said to him, "if you start at once can you get this boy to Monte Cassino by nightfall?"

"I think so, your ladyship."

"Then have three of the knights prepare themselves. You and Thomas will travel with an armed escort."

"Why an escort?" It was Thomas speaking. "We've always made the trip alone."

"Things have changed lately, Thomas. The country-side is dangerous now—thanks to our royal cousin."

"The wicked emperor?" Thomas clapped a hand to his mouth, wishing that he had not let the word "wicked" slip past his lips.

Theodora was staring at him. "Did I hear you correctly?" she inquired. "Are you calling His Imperial Highness . . . ?"

"I meant nothing."

"Where do you pick up such ideas? Who has been talking to you?"

"I have, my lady." Fellow spoke quietly from his position near the hall door.

"You!" Theodora regarded the varlet with blazing eyes.

"Forgive me, my lady. I meant no harm."

"No harm, eh? What have you been telling my son about the Emperor Frederick?"

"Just varlets' gossip, my lady."

"And what are the varlets saying?"

"Talk—nothing but talk."

"I am very much interested in hearing what others are saying. Go on, please."

"But, my lady! It's not for me to talk to you about the emperor."

"When I ask a question, Fellow, I expect an answer."

"Very well, my lady. I know only what everybody knows. The emperor has been thrown out of the Church."

From Thomas, standing by the big arm chair, came a gasp. "Oh, no", he murmured. "The poor man!"

His mother's eyes fell briefly on the boy's face. "Spare your tears, Thomas", she said sharply. "Your cousin Frederick is quite able to take care of himself." Her attention returned to the varlet. "So far so good, Fellow", she went on. "What you say is true. The emperor has been excommunicated. What else have you heard about him?"

"Only that he's fighting the Holy Father, my lady. People say the emperor is seizing lands that belong to the Church. They say his soldiers are attacking the monasteries, looting them, and killing innocent monks. They say the emperor won't rest until he has made himself boss of everything."

"Boss of everything!" Lady Theodora picked up Fellow's words with a harsh laugh. "And what does that expression mean, pray tell me?"

"Your ladyship knows what it means. Frederick isn't satisfied to rule the empire. He also wants to rule the Church of God itself!"

The countess moved away suddenly, going in the direction of the tall windows at the end of the room. Fellow's eyes followed her. "Perhaps", he murmured, "I shouldn't say these things in the presence of the boy."

The countess laughed again. "The boy will hear them sooner or later", she said. She turned back, her eyes on Thomas' troubled face. "Yes, Son," she continued, "you will hear many different things. You will hear people who think as Fellow does—that Frederick is a wicked, horrid person. Then, again, you will hear some say that he is the most gifted ruler in the history of mankind. Such people call him 'the wonder of the world'."

The countess' eyes lifted. For a moment she seemed to forget that there were others in the room. "The wonder of the world!" she whispered to herself, obviously relishing the words and agreeing with them. "And there are still other people . . ." Her voice trembled now with disapproval and contempt. "People who say the emperor is mad, insane."

Her gaze lowered, coming level with her son's eyes. "If you listen to these different opinions, Thomas, you will become terribly confused. So let me give you a piece of advice. Frederick is your liege lord and sovereign. We Aquinos have always been loyal to our liege lord. We always will be. Remember that. Whatever you hear about Frederick, good or bad, remember the loyalty you owe him—and forget the rest."

She swept toward the hall door. "All right, Fellow," she said, "you may pack the boy's things."

"Mother!" Thomas ran after her. "About those knights you're sending to guard us?"

"What about them?"

"Why do we need an armed escort?"

"Because Frederick has set up his camp near Monte Cassino. You know what that means. Wherever the emperor goes, he is followed by a multitude of low people. Camp followers they're called. Most of them are beggars, outlaws, or worse. If such people saw a young lord traveling with only one servant—well! You might be waylaid and robbed. You might even be killed."

"But they won't know I'm a young lord, Mother. I'll be wearing my habit. Besides, how will you get along?"

"I?"

"Yes. With a whole castle to protect, with Father and most of your knights fighting for the emperor, you need the knights that are here. I wouldn't feel right taking them from you."

"Wouldn't you!" Lady Theodora spoke sharply, but there was a touch of admiration in the glance she gave her son. "You would not be afraid to travel alone with Fellow under the circumstances?"

"Of course not."

"And you?" Theodora turned to the varlet. "How do you feel about it?"

"We have fast horses, my lady. I doubt if there's an outlaw in the kingdom with a horse that could catch us."

"And if some outlaws did?"

"I would die before I let them touch a hair of the boy's head."

"I believe you would." She smiled. "In fact, I believe you would guard him better than a dozen knights. Very well, then. Get yourself a sword from the storehouse. You and Thomas shall travel alone." She nodded at Fellow as he opened the door for her. She nodded at her son. "I will say good-bye, now, Thomas", she said. "Take care of yourself on the highroad."

3

"THE WONDER OF THE WORLD"

IT WAS ONLY SIX MILES to the Abbey of Monte Cassino. Even so, it was a lengthy journey by horseback because of the roughness of the mountain country. The highroad dipped through the village of Rocca Secca on the lowest slope of the castle hill. It ran between the fertile fields of the valley where the peasants of Rocca Secca cultivated their grain with hand plows and pickaxe-like mattocks. Eastward of the fields, the road rose slightly, twisting between ledges of gleaming rock.

It was late afternoon before Thomas and Fellow came within sight of the crossroad beyond which rose the seventeen-hundred-foot mountain on which the abbey stood. Behind them the hot sun lay close to the horizon. A stunted pine far out in a rocky field shed a long shadow.

For hours the boy and the man had ridden in silence. Neither was much of a talker, and the boy's mind was busy with the things his mother had said that morning. From time to time he glanced at his companion. He wondered if Fellow could answer the question in his mind.

"Fellow!" He decided finally to find out. "Why did the Holy Father excommunicate my cousin Frederick?"

Fellow's eyes were on the ledge to his right. "Haven't you heard enough about the emperor today?" he asked. "This fight between His Imperial Highness and the Pope. Ah, Master Thomas, that's a mixed-up story; and you're pretty young—perhaps too young—to understand it."

"If I don't understand it, Fellow, no harm done. If I do, then I'm not too young. Proceed."

Fellow proceeded. "Well, now, Master Thomas," he began, "once upon a time the great Emperor Frederick, he . . . Mind you, Master Thomas, all this happened many, many years ago."

"Yes, yes, Fellow. Go on."

"Well, then, as I was saying—the Emperor Frederick, he gave the Holy Father his solemn promise that as of such and such a date he would take his knights and his squires, his bowmen and his varlets, and he would go on a noble crusade to the Holy Land. Well, the days passed, and the months, and finally the day came, the day on which the emperor had promised to begin his crusade. And what do you think happened?"

"What?"

"Nothing! The emperor did not so much as budge from his palace. He simply sat on his throne twiddling his thumbs and making nasty remarks about the Holy Father. In short, Master Thomas . . ."

"In short," Thomas broke in, impatient with Fellow's roundabout way of telling a story, "the emperor broke his promise to the Holy Father. And then what?"

"Then more days passed, Master Thomas, and more months, and even years. And then one bright morning the emperor did take his knights and his squires, his bowmen and his varlets, and set forth on a crusade."

"At the Pope's request?"

"Oh, no, Master Thomas. The emperor simply set out for the Holy Land because he had a mind to. He suddenly felt like traveling. But when he arrived in the Holy Land an amazing thing happened."

Thomas' face was now one big wrinkle of doubt. He was beginning to wonder if Fellow might be making it all up. "How amazing?" he inquired.

"Well, Master Thomas, you know what a crusade is for. Once he got to the Holy Land, the emperor was supposed to fight the heathens—the Turkish and the Arabic infidels, that is. Instead, Master Thomas, he fell in love with them."

"Fell in love with the infidels?"

"So I'm told. He liked everything about them. He even became emancipated with their animals." Fellow paused, frowning in perplexity. "Am I using that word right, Master Thomas?"

"I think the word is 'infatuated'."

"Right you are. The emperor became infat—that is, he became fond of the infidels' animals. As you know, Master Thomas, the infidels live in Asia and Africa. Those countries are full of vast jungles, and the jungles are full of enormous animals. Animals, Master Thomas, the like of which you and I have never laid eyes on. And what do you know! The emperor became so infat—I mean he liked these animals so much that when he came home he brought hundreds and hundreds of them along. Now they say the emperor won't so much as cross the road without taking some of those strange beasts with him. Now what do you think of that, Master Thomas?"

"I think the Holy Father wouldn't excommunicate the emperor because he brought some silly old animals home from the Holy Land."

"Of course not. But the emperor brought something else home from the land of the infidels—something far worse."

"What, Fellow?"

"Ideas!" Fellow tapped his forehead and rolled his eyes. "Ideas, Master Thomas! Some people say the emperor isn't a Christian any more at all. They say he has adopted the religion of the infidels. He has become a Muslim!"

"A Muslim?" The word was by no means new to Thomas. He had heard it from time to time whispered among the Benedictine monks of Monte Cassino. He had no idea, however, what it meant.

Nor did Fellow really. Asked for an explanation, he waved his free hand one way and the hand holding the reins of his mount the other, and he tossed a jumble of meaningless words into the air. "But one thing I can tell you", he finished. "I can tell you what the Muslims do *not* believe." He bowed his head suddenly and with grave respect. "They do not believe in our Lord, Jesus Christ."

"And the emperor, Fellow? Doesn't he believe in our Lord now?"

Fellow gave his mustache a hefty pull. "I'm telling you only what I've heard people saying", he answered. "Nothing more. Nothing less."

Thomas studied the high-held head of the black gelding he was riding. He muttered something under his breath.

"Yes, Master Thomas?"

The boy smiled. "I guess I was talking to myself."

It was Fellow's turn to smile. It wasn't the first time he had caught his young master jabbering away to empty air.

"I was just wondering", Thomas added. "Would you say that Frederick was a happy man?"

"Good saints alive! Only you would think of that. What makes you ask?"

"From what you've said, it's hard to see how he could be."

They rode on in silence. All day the air had been unusually clear, every landmark standing out against a cloudless sky. In the drooping light of early evening the picture was changing. A gathering mist blurred rock into rock. Halfway up Monte Cassino, still a distance away, a lonely peasant's cabin on a gentle slope seemed one with the gray cliff behind it.

With a sudden jerking movement Fellow brought his horse to a halt. His outstretched arm signaled the boy to do likewise. Fellow rose in his stirrups. He leaned forward, peering southward in the direction of the crossroad.

Thomas followed his gaze. He could see nothing at first—nothing, that is, except a thick cloud rolling over the crossroad. Then he saw that the cloud was dust rising from the hoofs of horses of a small party of soldiers. Knights, apparently; he could see the gleam of their armor in the dying sunlight. Behind the knights came a far larger body of infantrymen moving on foot and carrying what seemed to be crossbows. And behind the bowmen . . .

"Fellow!" Thomas was high in his own stirrups now. "Do you see what I see?"

Fellow nodded. He had seen. Loping along behind the bowmen, almost comic in their lumbering dignity, were a score, or maybe two score, of tremendous animals. Thomas leaned away from his horse as far out as he could—farther, in fact, than was strictly safe. "Fellow!" he shouted. "It must be the emperor!"

Fellow was nodding vigorously. "If not the emperor," he grunted, "then some of his men escorting his beasts to camp. But what are they, Master Thomas? What name should a man put to such strange creatures?"

"Their names, Fellow? I'll tell you what they are. They're . . . !" Poor Thomas! He had spoken too soon. He realized suddenly that he had quite forgotten the name of those animals. It was his good friend at the abbey, Brother Bell Ringer, who had told him about them. Brother Bell Ringer had traveled in his youth. He had seen many things. For Thomas he had drawn a picture of one of those beasts—a great balloon of a creature with a little twist of a tail, huge flapping ears and, strangest of all, a curling trunk instead of a nose.

"Elephants!" The name came to Thomas suddenly, and he slapped it out with glee. "Elephants! That's what they are, Fellow. They're elephants! And those bigger animals behind, the ones with the ladders for necks—those are giraffes! Think of that, Fellow! Giraffes! Hurry, now! We'll stop at the crossroad and watch them go by."

He was already on his way, having slapped his horse into full speed. On his larger and faster horse, Fellow took after him. "Stop, master", he shouted. "Stop, I say!"

His horse came clattering alongside the boy's. He reached out, seizing the bridle of the other mount and jolting it to a standstill. "Have you lost your mind, Master Thomas?" he demanded. "The emperor's men may take us for enemies."

"But, Fellow, my father and brothers are with His Imperial Highness. We'll tell his men who we are."

"And maybe they'll believe us, Master Thomas. And maybe they won't. Maybe they'll take us off to the emperor's camp to find out."

"Wouldn't that be sort of fun?"

"Silence, young master. Whatever's got into you? Your mother told me to get you to Monte Cassino with all due speed. And there with all due speed I intend to get you. We'll see the emperor's beasts go by all right; but we'll see them where we can't be seen. Come along, now. Follow me!"

Fellow swerved his horse off the road. He rode through a break in the ledge and across the field with Thomas' horse cantering along behind. Fellow headed for a low embankment alongside the crossroad. There were some sharp outcroppings of rock there and one large boulder. Fellow tossed the reins of his horse over an outcropping behind the boulder and gestured to Thomas to do the same. He climbed onto the flat top of the boulder, with Thomas at his heels.

"We'll watch here where they can't see us", he whispered to the boy. "Down now and keep your head low."

Fellow had already flattened himself on the rock. Thomas stretched out beside him.

He saw at once that Fellow had chosen a perfect spot. They were well hidden, yes; but the road lay immediately below, only some ten feet away. True, they could not see the oncoming procession at this moment; but that was because of a sharp turn in the road about fifty feet to their right. But they would see it soon, Thomas knew. They would see the procession the minute it started coming around the rocky wall of the curve.

It came. First the knights, looking very handsome in their glistening coats of mail and high, conical helmets. And then the bowmen, a hundred strong. And then— the animals!

At his first close look at the elephants Thomas felt his breath leave him for a second. The huge beasts were not alone. A varlet trotted by the side of each, guiding his charge with gentle nudges of a long pole. What wonderfully shaped heads the elephants had and how wonderfully small and blinky-bright the eyes in those giant heads! As for the giraffes—to Thomas' way of thinking they were even more wonderful with their long, dipping necks and gentle faces, each with a rather startled expression as if the animal were as amazed at its own magnificence as Thomas and his varlet were.

"Beautiful!" Thomas thought. "Beautiful." The word forced itself to his lips. "Beautiful, beautiful!" he whispered, and he felt Fellow's hand on his mouth and saw Fellow's head shaking close to his. He put the sleeve of his black habit in his mouth to keep himself from further exclamations. He looked with amusement at Fellow, seeing that the varlet's eyes were as wide as his own— wide with pleasure and delight.

On and on the animals came. On and on. And then they were gone, out of sight beyond another curve in the crossroad to their left. And Thomas looked down into the empty road and sighed to see how empty it was!

He jumped to his feet, but Fellow pulled him down at once. Fellow pointed to the curve in the road. "There might be stragglers still coming, Master", he whispered. "Can you count?"

"Yes, Fellow. The monks taught me long ago."

"How far can you count?"

"To almost any number."

"Count whatever makes up a minute, then, and we'll leave."

Thomas counted slowly to sixty and got to his feet. Fellow rose. He climbed down from the boulder and headed for his horse. Thomas could not tear himself away so fast.

He looked again at the road below him. This time his mind filled it once more—filled it with the magnificent elephants, the even more magnificent giraffes.

He looked up at the sky. He was smiling and at the same time he was crying.

"Thank you, God", he said in a clear, quiet voice. "What beautiful things you have placed here to amaze and please us. How can anyone doubt you, O God; how can anyone doubt that you exist? The poor emperor, for example. O God, I beg you from the bottom of my heart—help His Imperial Highness to find his faith again!"

"Thank you, little monk!"

The voice that came up to Thomas from the roadbed below was as musical as any sound he had ever heard from the human throat. He looked down with a shiver. He had not realized how thin the fading evening light had become. Then, too, his eyes were still misty with tears. It was a second before he realized that there were four mounted figures below—three men and a small boy!

One of the men laughed as Thomas' eyes fell on him. Thomas knew at once, from the musical quality of the laugh, that he was the man who had spoken.

He was a tall, slender man astride a beige-colored war horse. Thomas' glance took in the luminous, yet brooding, quality of his dark eyes, the imperial emblem on his armor. He knew at once who it was. He was staring into the strange, strong face of Frederick the Second, his cousin on both sides of the family, king of Sicily, king of Jerusalem, king of Germany, emperor of the Holy Roman Empire and "wonder of the world"!

4

A WHISPERED WARNING

WHEN, IN THE YEAR 1239, Frederick the Second brought his army to a camp near Monte Cassino, he was forty-five years old. He had the vigor of a much younger man and a face that could be any age. When he was pleased, His Imperial Highness looked like a youth.

Clouded by displeasure or by anger, his sharp features became those of a man who had lived a thousand years.

The emperor's family name was Hohenstaufen.

His grandfather Frederick Barbarossa—Frederick of the Red Beard—had been among the most famous of all the Holy Roman Emperors.

Like his grandfather, Frederick the Second had a brilliant mind. He was not only a ruler and a lawmaker of skill, he was an artist, a scientist, and the author of a book on hawks and other birds that would become a classic.

Like his grandfather, he had an attractive personality. And again like his grandfather, he displayed at times a highly unattractive character.

He was born and brought up in Palermo, then the seacoast capital of the kingdom of Sicily. When he was three years old, his emperor-father died. Overnight Frederick became king of Sicily, a country that, in those days, comprised the island of Sicily and sections of southern Italy, including the city of Naples and the area where Rocca Secca stood.

Three-year-old Frederick, of course, was too young to rule. His mother and an uncle did so for him. The times were troubled; his mother and uncle had many enemies, and the boy's life was difficult. He lived in a palace of many rooms filled with art treasures. But rooms and statues cannot be eaten, and there were times when the boy-king of Sicily had scarcely enough to eat. Nor can rooms and statues be worn, and there were times when the boy-king's clothes were as thin and tattered as those of a beggar.

When he was fourteen, Frederick became king of Sicily on his own. Four years later, he was also crowned king of Germany. Nine years after that, while he was traveling in the Holy Land on his crusade, he was crowned king of Jerusalem.

His most important position, however, was that of emperor of the Holy Roman Empire, a position he was given in 1220 at the age of twenty-six. The Holy Roman Empire was founded in 962 and ended in 1806. It was a sort of United Nations, made up of half a dozen or more countries in western Europe. All these countries were Christian, so they banded together to form what they thought of as a holy empire. To guide the empire they elected an emperor. They liked to think of their emperor as the vicar of God on earth where political and economic matters were concerned, just as the Pope is the vicar of God on earth where spiritual matters are concerned.

Such was the background of the man into whose face Thomas found himself looking in the fading light of that evening in 1239. In his confusion and surprise, the boy forgot his manners. He neither bent his knee to the emperor nor inclined his head. He simply stared.

He stared first at Frederick himself and then at the two men who were with him. He had no idea who the others were. He assumed from the proud way they sat on their horses that they were men of importance in the emperor's court.

His gaze rested longest on the fourth member of the party. He was a small boy, considerably younger than Thomas. He wore a pair of long scarlet hose or, rather, tights, a hip-length jacket trimmed with fur, and the soft, flat hat of a page. He met Thomas' stare with a friendly nod. His smile was no less appealing because two of his baby teeth had recently departed and the new ones had not yet grown in.

It took Thomas only a second to cast his eyes over the group below. In that second, having heard voices on the crossroad, Fellow had scrambled back up the boulder. Fellow had no idea who the strangers were. He knew only that his young master had been sighted. His young master, therefore, was in danger. In one and the same movement, he pushed Thomas roughly behind him, seized the long sword at his side, and flourished it in the air.

"Stay where you are!" he cried. "My young master is the son of one of the noblest lords in Italy. Whoever touches him will have myself to reckon with!"

There was a chuckle below. It came from the emperor. "Neatly spoken, varlet", he said in his low, pleasant voice. "Neatly spoken. But tell me, my good man, have you the dimmest idea of how to use that sharp weapon in your hand?"

"Try me, sir. Try me and see!"

Thomas was tugging at his varlet's sleeve. "Not 'sir'!" he whispered. "Sire!"

"Sire!" Fellow's eyes bulged. Only emperors and kings,

he knew, were addressed as "sire". He fell to his knees, the point of his sword clattering on the rock beside him.

The emperor was still smiling. "Rise, varlet", he commanded. "So our little monk is also a little lord. Step forth, little lord monk. Let me have a closer look."

Thomas moved to the edge of the rock immediately above the emperor. He could feel the sharpness of Frederick's gaze.

"I am not yet a monk", Thomas told him. "I am merely an oblate and a student under the Benedictines at the Abbey of Monte Cassino."

"And that is where you are bound, little lord? You are on your way to Monte Cassino?"

"Yes, Your Majesty."

The emperor turned slightly in his saddle. He cast a frowning glance at one of his companions. Later Thomas would recall that glance. Later, too, he would know the meaning of it.

The emperor had addressed him again. "What is your name, little lord?"

"I am the son of the lord of Aquino, Sire. They call me Thomas Aquinas."

The emperor nodded vigorously. "But of course, of course. I should have known. Your father, that great warrior, and your brothers have told me much about you. They tell me you are different. They say you are a thinker. They say that some day you will adorn some high place in the Church."

"With this chubby figure, Sire, I doubt if I am ever much of an adornment anywhere."

The emperor's head flew back. His musical laugh filled the air. He brought his head forward suddenly, staring at Thomas with a strange light in his eyes. "Little lord," he said, "you were praying when I arrived. Do you think God hears our prayers?"

"I am sure he does."

"Does he answer them?"

"Always, Sire—provided we ask for the things it is right and good for us to have."

"Has he answered the prayer you were making when I first spoke to you?"

"Yes, Sire."

"And what was his answer?"

"I do not know."

"You do not know!" The emperor shook his head. "I must speak to your Benedictine instructors. They have not taught you to make sense."

"In what way, Sire, have I failed to make sense?"

"First you tell me God has answered your prayer. Then you say you do not know what the answer was. If you have the answer, you must know what it is."

"Not necessarily, Sire. Are you acquainted with the science of arithmetic?"

"I have studied it long and hard."

"Have you ever looked up the answer to a difficult problem in arithmetic, only to discover that you did not understand the answer?"

"Many times."

"Did you then decide that the answer had never been made simply because you did not understand it?"

"Of course not. I simply decided that I was not smart enough to understand."

"So it is with the answers to our prayers, Sire. The fact that we are seldom smart enough to understand them does not mean that God has not answered. After all, the knowledge of the wisest man on earth is nothing compared with the knowledge of God, who is Wisdom itself."

The emperor's eyebrows had lifted as Thomas spoke. "Well, well, well," he muttered as the boy finished, "you have a good mind, Thomas Aquinas. Now satisfy my curiosity about one other thing. How come I found you here, a few minutes ago, standing on a boulder at the foot of Monte Cassino and saying a prayer in my behalf? What have you heard about me, Thomas Aquinas?"

"Something that distresses me, Imperial Highness."

"What?"

"That you no longer believe that Jesus Christ is truly God."

"You have heard correctly. I now believe that Jesus was a great man but still a mere man. What do you say to that, Thomas Aquinas?"

"I crave His Imperial Highness' permission to ask him another question."

"Ask away."

"You have been kind enough, Sire, to say that I have a

good mind. Suppose, now, I look you straight in the eye. Suppose I say to you, in all seriousness, that I am God. What would you call me then?"

"I would call you a faker and a fool."

"Would you not call any mere man a faker and fool if he claimed to be God?"

"I would."

"Then how can you say Christ was merely human and at the same time call him a great man, in view of the fact that he himself several times said he was God?"

Thomas, ceasing to speak, could hear his words echoing against the rock on the far side of the crossroad. There was a silence of some seconds. Then the emperor spoke again.

"I wish we had more time to discuss these things, Thomas Aquinas. Alas, you have a long climb to Monte Cassino ahead of you. And I have a long journey to camp. So we must part—but with the great hope that we will meet again someday."

Thomas noticed that whatever His Imperial Highness did, the two men with him did. When the emperor frowned, they frowned. The emperor was smiling now, so they were smiling.

The little page had gotten down from his horse. Boy-like, he had picked up some rocks and was tossing them, one by one, down the road. Glancing up at the emperor, he gave his last rock a careless fling. It sailed close to the head of the emperor's horse, and the handsome beast shied suddenly.

Immediately a great change came over the face of Frederick the Second, a change that left Thomas amazed and shocked. All charm fled from the emperor's features, all light from his eyes.

"Do you see what that young scoundrel of a page boy has done?" he cried to the man on his right. "Seize him the minute we reach camp. Turn him over to two strong varlets. Instruct them to whip him. Do you hear me? The boy is to be whipped within an inch of his life!"

"Oh, no, Your Imperial Highness!" For the first time Thomas was on his knees to the emperor. "Please, Majesty", he begged. "The boy meant no harm. It was an accident. Take back your order. I ask it as a boon. I ask it as an Aquino, as a kinsman of three of your most loyal knights!"

Another silence. Thomas looked up slowly. To his relief he saw that the emperor was his old self once more. He was nodding. "I admire the grace of your speech, Thomas Aquinas," he said quietly, "and the generosity of your heart. Do not fret yourself further. Your boon is granted. The page boy will not be whipped." The emperor smiled. Out of the corner of his eye, Thomas could see the page boy mounting his horse. He, too, was smiling. "And now", he heard the emperor saying, "I must bid you a last farewell."

Fellow, too, had dropped to his knees. Together the boy and the varlet watched the emperor and his party gallop away. They disappeared around the curve. Soon the echoes of their horses' hoofs could be heard no more.

Fellow climbed down from the boulder and hastened to his mount. "Hurry, now, Master Thomas", he called over his shoulder. "We must make speed. We must take advantage of what little daylight remains to us."

Without further speech they galloped down the cross-road and into the highroad. At an increasingly slower pace they began the difficult ascent of the mountain on which the ancient Abbey of Monte Cassino stood.

The evening light was going fast. Only a little remained when their ears picked up the sound of a horseman approaching at their rear. The road at this point was a narrow ledge, overshadowed by the face of the mountain itself.

"Into the shadows, Master Thomas", Fellow whispered sharply. "We'll wait here and see who it is. One never knows."

They did not have long to wait. Thomas was the first to recognize the oncoming horseman. "The page boy!" he shouted. "It's the emperor's page boy, Fellow."

The page boy's horse, driven at top speed up the mountain road, was wringing wet. The animal's flanks quivered as it came abreast of them, and its young rider reined to a stop.

The page boy, too, was exhausted from the fast ride up the hill. Or, perhaps, his exhaustion stemmed from excitement over the message he had come to deliver. At any rate he found it impossible to lift his voice above a whisper. His words came in a steam-like hiss.

"Master Thomas, you saved me from a beating", he

began, sliding his words together in his haste. "I've come to return the favor, after which I must hurry back before I'm missed. The emperor—the emperor and his men—they plan to attack the Abbey of Monte Cassino. Maybe tonight, maybe tomorrow night."

The boy hissed out his last word, wheeled his horse away from them, and was gone. He had disappeared down the hill before Thomas or Fellow could speak a word.

In the gathering darkness the boy and the man faced one another. Then, in a tense silence, they mounted their horses and spurred them upward along the narrow mountain road. Night had come in earnest, a dark night only faintly lighted by a crescent moon. Fortunately, their mounts had made the journey many times. They carried their anxious riders, almost without guidance, to the flat summit of the hill.

The Abbey of Monte Cassino was even larger than the castle of Rocca Secca. Half a dozen stone buildings and again as many wooden structures crouched together within its low walls. Fellow dismounted and opened the unguarded gates. A single lantern punctured the gloom of the front courtyard. In the huge main building, the building where the monks lived, two more lanterns made a shadowy tunnel of the center hall.

Hurrying down the hall with Fellow, Thomas could hear the slap-slap of his sandals on the cement floor. He pounded on the door of Father Abbot's quarters.

The door was opened at once, and Father Abbot

regarded his visitors in the yellow light streaming from the candle on his desk. He was an old man, very tall, with a strong, handsome face. "Ah," he said, "it's you, Master Thomas. Welcome home." He paused, a frown clouding his deep-set eyes. "Is anything wrong?" he asked, looking from Thomas to Fellow and back again.

Thomas told him. In a tumble of words he described their encounter with the emperor. He told Father Abbot how the page boy had come after them. He repeated the page boy's whispered warning.

His heart sank as he saw Father Abbot slowly nodding his head. "I have been afraid of this", the old priest murmured. He glanced at Fellow.

"You," he said, "you know where the prior's cell is. Awaken him, please, and tell him to come to me at once."

Fellow was on his way. "As for you, Master Thomas . . ." Father Abbot smiled at the boy. "I must ask you to go quietly to your cell. Go to bed, please, as though nothing unusual were afoot." His thin hand dropped on Thomas' shoulder. "And don't forget your prayers", he added. "If it's God's will that the emperor attack, we must rely on God's love to protect us."

The schoolhouse stood on the far side of the court behind the main building. Thomas' cell was scarcely wider than the reach of his two arms. There was a wooden desk, a stool, and a straw-filled pallet on the stone floor. The boy sank to his knees before the crucifix on the wall. Earnestly he asked God's protection for

Monte Cassino. Once more he asked him to help the Emperor Frederick regain his lost faith.

He flung himself on his pallet, still wearing his habit. His mind was in a turmoil, busy with all that had happened during the last few hours, even busier with what might happen before the night was gone. Thomas was convinced that simple nervousness would never allow him to sleep. He reckoned, however, without the tiring strain of the day's events. Closing his eyes, he fell asleep at once.

He awakened some two hours later with equal suddenness. His first thought was that the light at the window of his cell was the light of dawn. Then he realized that no dawn had ever blazed so red.

Never in his memory had the halls and courtyards of Monte Cassino echoed with such din and confusion.

He ran to the window. Almost all of the wooden structures within view were burning. The rest, he saw, were being set afire by pine torches flung over the walls of the monastery.

Throwing open the door of his cell, he stepped into the path of a score of fleeing boys. Only a quick step back avoided a collision. He could see the boys crowding through an entrance down the hall, a narrow archway to the steps leading to the catacomb-like cellars of the monastery. Another boy, running after the others, stopped long enough to yell something at him—something that Thomas did not catch. Far away, in the front courtyard, he could hear the shouts of men, the scream-

ing of frightened horses, the relentless thud of a battering ram as the soldiers of Frederick the Second pounded
open the doors and poured into the main building of the
Abbey of Monte Cassino!

5

BROTHER BELL RINGER

WITHIN SECONDS after opening his door, Thomas was alone in the dimly lit hall. His first thought was to follow the other students. Off the cellar, he knew, was a long tunnel. The tunnel had been built for purposes of escape. It ran under the monastery walls and came out fully half a mile away onto a slope of the mountain itself.

He had taken only a few steps, however, when another and more powerful thought stopped him.

Fellow! Fellow would be sleeping in the servants' wing of the visitors' house on the far side of the paved court behind the main building. The varlets with him might not know about the escape tunnel.

He turned, heading for the courtyard door. Reaching the end of the corridor, he opened the door carefully. He closed it with a gasp. Soldiers! There were soldiers out there. He could see them milling about under their lanterns and pine torches. Only one possible route to the visitors' house remained—a long passageway opening off the hall to his right.

It was dark in the passageway. Moreover, there were several turns. He had to proceed slowly, feeling for the turns with outstretched arms. Once he stopped, under the impression that footsteps were coming his way. He listened hard, holding his breath. The sound came again, but now it seemed to come from above. Soldiers of the emperor, quite likely; but if so, they must be in the corridors of the second floor. He moved on. Beyond the next turn the passageway widened. Windows here and there let in a little light. He could go faster now. He started to run. He was barely under way when, from somewhere in the darkness to his side, a hand reached out, seizing his arm and jolting him to a halt. A second jolting movement pulled him into the shadows of an alcove.

Another hand, clamped over his mouth, stifled the cry that sprang to his lips. He would have struggled to free himself but just then he saw a light creeping along the passageway floor. He froze, watching the light with fascinated eyes. It was obviously from a lantern. It was coming closer now, and closer, carving an ever-wider swathe of dull yellow along the stone floor.

Five soldiers trooped by, bowmen all of them, in long black hose and short coats of mail. The lantern was in the hand of the rearmost man. The man stopped suddenly not five feet from the alcove. He hoisted the lantern above his head, turning slowly and looking slowly around. For a terrified second Thomas was certain that, in the next second, he would find himself squarely in the path of the light. But, as suddenly as he had stopped, the man walked on, lowering his lantern.

Above the flap of the retreating footsteps Thomas could hear a voice at his ear. "Quiet, boy. We—we—we—we'll stay here till we—we—we—we're sure they've gone."

The words came in a low whisper, but Thomas knew at once who it was. Who else stuttered in the monastery? He threw his arms around the frail figure at his side. "Oh, Brother Bell Ringer!" he gasped.

He could hear Brother Bell Ringer clearing his throat. He was struggling to bring out his next whisper. "Wh—wh—wh—what are you doing here, boy? Why aren't you fleeing wi—wi—wi—with the other students?"

"Fellow!" Thomas whispered. "He brought me here this evening, and he's spending the night in the visitors' house. I was afraid he might not know about the escape tunnel."

"Don't worry about Fellow. He can take care of himself if anyone can. We'll go now. We—we—we—we'll go to the bell tower and hide in the closet off the tower platform."

"But won't the soldiers search the tower?"

"If they do, we're out of luck. But my guess is they've already searched it, in whi—whi—whi—which case we'll be safe. Here. Let me guide you. I could run through these corridors blindfolded."

Brother Bell Ringer knew the corridors all right. Thomas, holding onto his hand, had to exert himself to keep up. Brother Bell Ringer's swift, gliding stride belied his seventy-plus years. Down one long hallway they sped, across another, and through a small door into a remote corner of the courtyard. There, stooping low, they made their way through the deep shadow of a boxwood hedge.

They slipped into the vestibule of the church and from there into the windowless room at the foot of the bell tower. The old monk guided Thomas to the ladder. In spite of the darkness, Thomas could see his uplifted finger. Thomas raised his head. Far above, a faint gray light sifting through the openings in the tower balcony showed the platform above which the great bells hung.

"Up with you, now", he heard Brother Bell Ringer whispering. "Up with you and . . ." The hissing sound of the old monk's voice ceased briefly. "Listen!" he whispered.

Thomas had already heard the footsteps on the court-yard outside. "Soldiers, Brother Bell Ringer?" he asked.

"Quite likely. But don't worry. I'll bar the doors to either side of us here. Up the ladder with you now."

"But aren't you coming with me?"

"Of course. As soon as I've barred the doors. Hurry now, and don't forget the closet off the platform. The minute you're inside, close the closet door. Do you hear me, boy? Close the door of the closet behind you. Hurry now. Up with you. Up!"

Thomas climbed as speedily as he could. It was a long ladder, supported only by the edge of the high platform to which it led. It swayed somewhat under Thomas' weight. He climbed steadily, keeping his head up, his eyes fixed on the faint gray light above.

In spite of the open slits high in the balcony, it was hard to see anything on the platform itself. Thomas had to feel around for the closet. It was some time before the wall finally gave under his hands and he realized that he had found the door. He pushed it open and crawled in.

He had no sooner closed the closet door behind him than he understood why Brother Bell Ringer had made such a point of his doing so.

The bells began to ring! Even with the thick door muffling the sound, the clang of the bells so close at hand sent the blood to his head with a stab of pain. He stopped his ears with his hands. It did no good. The pain only increased. The floor shook beneath him, and he felt that at any moment the pain would split his head in two.

Then the bells ceased ringing.

For a second he was conscious only of an almost unbearable relief. The blood left his head. The pain gradually died away. He could think again now. He could think—and wonder!

Why? Whatever had possessed the old monk to ring the bells at this moment? Or had he been forced to ring them? Had the soldiers perhaps . . . ?

Thomas cracked open the closet door. He listened. He could just make out a murmur far below—one voice, two, several voices! He crept to the edge of the ladder opening. He could see nothing clearly down below—nothing but thick shadows with still thicker shadows moving among them. Soldiers no doubt—soldiers crowding around Brother Bell Ringer.

Then, above the murmurs, he heard the old monk speaking. His voice was high-pitched, but amazingly calm and without a trace of stutter. "There", Thomas heard him declare. "I've rung the bells. There's no need for you to search the tower. No one could stay up there with those bells clanging in his ears."

A voice answered him, a gruff voice pitched too low for the words to reach the listening boy. Then it seemed to Thomas that the shadows below all blended into one. There was a shuffling sound, a series of shuffling sounds. Then the huge shadow broke into smaller ones; and then there were no shadows at all. Somewhere in the near distance a door rumbled shut. After that there was nothing at all—nothing but darkness and silence.

Thomas waited. Once he started to call Brother Bell Ringer's name but thought better of it. He reached for a rung of the ladder with his foot and started down. The descent was harder than the climb up had been. He had to proceed slowly, feeling for every rung with his foot. He wondered all the while what he would find below. He feared the worst.

First one foot and then the other touched the floor. He stood a second, trying to make out objects in the darkness. The first thing to come into focus was the bell rope. It was still swaying.

He moved toward it and bumped into something on the floor. He fell to his knees. It was Brother Bell Ringer. He could feel blood on the old monk's habit. He remembered stories his father had told him, stories of death on the battlefield. He remembered something his father had told him to do. He held his hand above the old man's mouth and nostrils. There was no breath.

Brother Bell Ringer was dead. The soldiers had killed him in cold blood!

Thomas fell on his friend's body with a gagging sob. He tried to silence himself, knowing that the soldiers might still be in the area. But the loud sobs came in spite of his efforts. He couldn't stop them. It was plain now what had happened. Brother Bell Ringer had been surprised by the soldiers as he went to bar the doors. They had threatened to search the tower, and he had stopped them by ringing the bells. He had saved Thomas' life in this way—and then the soldiers had cruelly taken his.

Thomas' sobs continued until there was no more in him. Then, somewhat calmer, he remembered something else his father had told him to do. He reached out his hand and gently closed the old monk's eyes.

Getting to his feet, he felt his way out of the bell-tower room, across the vestibule, and into the church itself. His eyes, accustomed to darkness, blinked briefly in the soft glow of the altar candles. The candlelight where it touched the floor made puddles of ruby red and green among its beautiful mosaics. Thomas, collapsing to his knees, did not at first have the strength to form words. But in time some little strength returned and he prayed for Brother Bell Ringer. From this position, spent with emotion, he suddenly crumpled to the floor, unconscious.

6

A FAMILY TALK

WHEN THOMAS' EYES opened again, he found himself looking into what seemed to be a blue haze. In a vague and confused way he remembered being in the church. He had fallen asleep, he figured. Now it must be morning, and the haze before him must be the sun shining through the stained-glass windows.

Then he realized that it was not a haze he was looking at. It was the filmy blue curtain that was sometimes dropped from the canopy of his bed. He was not in the church at Monte Cassino. He was home! He was in his own bed in his own bedroom at the castle of Rocca Secca!

Beyond the curtain he could hear voices—his mother's and then the guttural, growling bass of his big brother Landulph. His bed was huge. He edged himself to one side and parted the filmy curtains.

His mother and Landulph were talking in the alcove at one of the windows. They were facing each other, seated on the two settles that stood there. In a nearby corner of the big room he could see Fellow. Sitting on a small bench, Fellow had planted his elbows on his bony knees. He had lowered his head, resting it on upturned palms. Thomas' eyes traveled to the fireplace. There, tapping his long fingers on the mantel, which came even with his head, was his brother Ronald.

Thomas pushed the curtains farther apart. The movement brought his mother and Landulph to their feet. Ronald turned. Only Fellow, fast asleep in his corner, remained as he was.

Lady Theodora was dressed in her usual manner—a short silken tunic over her long robe-like gown, a gown known as a pelisse. Its heavy folds quivered as she hurried across the room. "Thomas, my dear!" She bent forward, doing something that she had not done in many years; she held his face between her hands and kissed him. "Are you all right?"

Thomas could only stare at her, puzzled. His gaze shifted. Beyond her he could see his brother Landulph grinning at him. Landulph was a bear of a man. Like Thomas, he had his father's broad shoulders and barrel chest. Unlike Thomas, his huge frame was all bones and muscle.

He was chuckling as he followed his mother across the room. "Answer the question, lad!" he shouted. Seizing Thomas' hand, he wrapped his own great paw around it. "Are you all right? May the saints preserve us if we haven't been waiting half the night and half the day to find out."

"I'm all right, Landulph. Only—only, what happened?"

"What happened indeed!" No one could drag his words out in a more irritating drawl than Thomas' brother Ronald. He pulled away from the fireplace as he spoke. Ronald was a tall, slender young man, slightly younger than Landulph. He had his mother's features, but he had not inherited her good looks. There was something dead about his eyes, something waxen about his lean cheeks and tight mouth.

Neither he nor Landulph was in battle dress. Their clothes this morning were much like their mother's. Landulph's pelisse hung every which way, as though he had jumped into it. It was otherwise with Ronald. His fur-lined pelisse was neatly cut and carefully draped. His headdress was a gold coronet. His black curls were heavily pomaded. They showed evidence of having received the attentions of a patient hairdresser.

He stopped near the bed, fingering the golden locket

around his neck. Bewildered as he was, Thomas could not help but be a little amused at Ronald. He loved all the members of his large family, but there were times when he had to work hard at loving Ronald. Ronald was such a fop, such a vain man. He had a sharp tongue and a quick temper.

He was staring at Thomas now, staring and fingering his locket. "Whatever got into you last night?" he demanded. "All the other students had the sense to flee when the attack came. So did the monks. But you—you would have to fly to the chapel and waste time mumbling your prayers."

"Hold now, Brother!" Landulph, coming to Ronald's side, punched him playfully in the ribs.

Ronald winced at the blow. He frowned. "What do you mean, Landulph? Hold what?"

"Don't scold the boy until you know what you're talking about. I'm sure Thomas had his reasons for remaining in the monastery." He turned to Thomas with a grin. "Did you not, my boy?"

"Why, yes, Landulph, I had good reasons. But that wasn't my question. What happened after I reached the monastery church? Who brought me here?"

"We did."

"You!"

"Your brother and I. Your brother and I and Fellow, I should say." Landulph nodded toward the distant corner of the room where Fellow sat, still dead to the world. "Fellow left through the escape tunnel", he continued. "Then he saw that you weren't with the others, so he went back. He found you in the church and brought you to us."

"And where were you—you and Ronald?"

Landulph started to reply, but his mother spoke first. "You know where they were, Thomas", she snapped. "You know that your brothers and your father have placed themselves under the command of the emperor."

"And they took part in the attack on Monte Cassino?"

"Yes, my son. They obeyed their emperor's orders. They took part in the attack!"

Thomas was sitting bolt upright now. He threw his legs over the bed. He was thinking of past things—of things that had puzzled him for many years. He remembered a time in his early childhood, an event that had taken place before he had ever set foot in the Abbey of Monte Cassino. His father had left the castle one day at the head of a body of knights. His father had led his knights to the abbey and had attacked it!

And now—now his father and his brothers had once more taken part in an attack on the ancient monastery.

Why? Why were the men of his family fighting on the side of the emperor against the Holy Father?

How many times he had asked himself that question. How many times he had let it go unspoken, half afraid of the answer that might come. He would ask it now. He would insist on an explanation.

"How could you?" he said, looking directly at Landulph. "How could you bring yourself to attack an unarmed monastery?"

"We had good reasons. There were spies hiding in the monastery."

"Spies?"

Landulph nodded. "Spies", he repeated. "Spies in the service of the Pope."

"How do you know this?"

"It is common knowledge."

"Maybe it is common knowledge to you." Thomas almost laughed. "Maybe it's common knowledge to Mother too, and to Ronald and the emperor. But I—I who have been a student at Monte Cassino since I was five years old, I who have lived there most of my life, I never saw any spies. I never saw anyone there, anyone but simple, God-fearing monks. How could you, Landulph? How could you come with your battering rams and your battle axes and your crossbows? How could you pound down the abbey doors and put innocent monks to the sword?"

"No monks were killed!" It was Ronald's voice, Ronald's spun-out, irritating drawl. He stepped a little closer to the bed. "All of them escaped", he declared. "All of them."

"One of them didn't!" Thomas shook his head vigorously. "Brother Bell Ringer didn't."

Lady Theodora was watching her youngest son with half-closed eyes. "Brother Bell Ringer?" she asked. "Who is Brother Bell Ringer?"

"Not 'is', Mother; 'was'." Thomas took a deep breath. "Brother Bell Ringer was one of the sweetest and kindest men who ever lived. I wouldn't be here this morning if it weren't for him. He hid me in the tower. And when the soldiers came he rang the bells so they wouldn't search for me. He saved my life. And the soldiers of the emperor—those big, brave brutes—they killed the poor old monk. They killed him on the spot!"

Thomas ceased speaking, choked by tears.

Landulph had dropped to his knees by the bed. He reached out his arms, but Thomas pulled away from his brother's embrace. "I'm sorry, boy." Landulph was trying hard to soften his rough voice. "Some of the soldiers must have just lost their heads. Believe me, lad, it was not our plan to kill any of the monks. Our orders were simply to take possession of the monastery in the emperor's name."

"But why, Landulph? Why?"

"Well, Thomas . . ."

Landulph got no further. Ronald had taken still another step toward the bed. "Why bother explaining anything, Landulph?" he asked impatiently. "Thomas is too young to understand. He hasn't brains enough to understand anyhow. There's nothing in that head of his but Our Fathers and Hail Marys and those silly psalms he's forever learning. I tell you the boy's an idiot, a brainless, stupid idiot!"

Landulph leaped to his feet. He confronted his elegantly dressed brother. Landulph was a good-natured man, but at the moment the heavy muscles of his face were squirming with anger. "Hold it, Ronald!" he thundered. "The boy has a right to ask questions. As for the names you've just called him, take them back. Take them back, I tell you!

"Take them back or, the saints preserve us, I'll ram them down your throat with my own fist!"

"Enough!" Lady Theodora had stepped between her two older sons. She, too, was angry, but her face was without emotion.

She looked at neither of them. Her eyes were on the moldings of the coffered ceiling. "Leave the room, both of you", she ordered. "If there are any explanations to be made to Thomas, I'll make them. Go now. Go in peace. There is enough fighting in this sad world without brother fighting brother."

They went—Landulph shamefacedly, Ronald with a sneer curving the corners of his mouth.

There was a silence. For some time Lady Theodora stood where she was, staring at the deeply sunken panels of the ceiling. When she lowered her eyes, Thomas saw that there were tears in them.

He held out his hand toward her as she approached. With a slight shake of her head she walked past him and sat down in the chair she had occupied the day before— the chair that swallowed her up. She sighed. She glanced briefly at Fellow, still snoozing in his corner.

"Thomas," she said, "there are questions you should not ask until you are quite certain you are old enough to understand the answers."

"I am quite certain I'm old enough, Mother. The question is—do you think I am?"

Theodora looked at him for a second. "I'm beginning to", she said. "Thomas, your father holds his lands of the emperor. Do you understand that expression?"

"I think I do."

Theodora uttered a faint, laughing sound. "When I was your age," she said, "I, too, thought I understood it, but I didn't really. All it amounts to is that the emperor is your father's liege lord and protector. In other words, we are all part and parcel of what is called the *feudal system*. Are you familiar with that expression?"

"In a dim sort of way."

"It is time for you to understand it in a not so dim way. You see, Thomas, the emperor permits your father to own and hold this castle. He also permits him to own and hold our other properties—the fortress in the village of Rocca Secca, our house in the town of Aquino, and the smaller castle there. This is not all the emperor has done for us. He has also given your father a solemn promise. If any of our properties are ever attacked, the emperor will bring his army and help us protect them."

There was a brief silence while Lady Theodora took the scented handkerchief from her sleeve and touched it to her forehead. "In return for all these kindnesses on the part of His Imperial Highness," she said, "your father has agreed to fight for him whenever that seems necessary. Now do you understand why he and your brothers are fighting on the emperor's side?"

"I sort of understand, Mother, only. . ."

"Only?"

"What about right and wrong? What if the Emperor Frederick is fighting on the wrong side?"

"Oh, Thomas!" His mother's words were one long sigh. "As you grow older you will see that it is sometimes very difficult to know what is right and what is wrong."

Thomas bit his lips. His mother's words brought to life a thought he had had many times before. It seemed to him that most of the time it was easy enough to see the difference between right and wrong. The trouble with many grownups was that they didn't always want to see the difference. They had a way of getting right and wrong all mixed up with what they wanted to do or didn't want to do. Sometimes, if they wanted to do something badly enough, they simply announced that it was right, even though it was not.

He was on the verge of speaking to his mother about this puzzling matter. Then he decided not to. His words would only distress her, and he could see that she was distressed enough already. With a long sigh of his own he let the whole matter drop.

Looking up, he saw that Theodora was smiling at him. "Thomas," she said, "I believe the time has come for us to discuss a very important matter. What do you want to be when you grow up?"

"To be? I guess I've never thought about it much."

"Well, let's think about it now. It's plain you'll never be a knight-warrior like Landulph or Ronald. Your father and I have hoped you might work in the Church. Would you like that?"

"Oh, yes, Mother. I'd love to be a monk like Brother Bell Ringer."

"Wonderful!" Theodora left her chair. She paced slowly across a section of the big room and back again. "Wonderful!" There was no sigh in her voice now. She was herself again, firm and to the point. "Then I'll tell you what we're going to do. Naturally you can't go back to Monte Cassino."

"Why not?"

"Because the monks are scattered. They will be until all this blows over. Besides, I have Father Abbot's word for it that you've learned all you can at the abbey school. So tomorrow morning Fellow and I will take you to Naples and get you settled there."

"At the University of Naples?"

"That's right, Thomas. You will study under some of the greatest scholars on earth. And when you are finished with your education . . ." Theodora had stopped in the center of the room, her hands tightly clasped in front of her slender waist. "Then you will come back. You will return to Monte Cassino."

"Good, Mother."

"Meanwhile," Theodora continued, "your father and I will have seen the proper people. After all, your father does have influence. Yes, Thomas, you will return to Monte Cassino; you will return as abbot!"

"Abbot!"

"Abbot of Monte Cassino."

"But, Mother . . ."

"Thomas!" Lady Theodora whirled on her son, suddenly aware that her words were not pleasing to him. "What's wrong with you? What are you trying to tell me?"

"That I don't want to be an abbot!"

"What?" She spoke with such sharpness that Fellow awakened on his bench in the corner and fell with a clatter to the floor. If her ladyship heard his grunts and mutters as he picked himself up, she gave no sign.

She stared fiercely at her son. "Thomas," she said in a low and level voice, "have you any idea who the abbot of Monte Cassino is?"

"Of course, Mother. I've often talked with him."

"I'm not talking about the man. I'm talking about the position. I'm talking about the position you will take over after you've finished your education at Naples." Lady Theodora was pacing the room again. "For your information," she continued, "the abbot of Monte Cassino is an important man. He is the superior of his order. He runs many monasteries. Furthermore, he is a quasi bishop, with other bishops under him."

"I know all that, but . . ."

"But what!" Theodora had come to a halt again in the center of the room.

"I don't mean to be disrespectful, but sometimes I don't think you listen to me. You must not have listened a few minutes ago."

"What did you say a few minutes ago?"

"I said I'd like to be a simple monk like Brother Bell Ringer."

"And what did Brother Bell Ringer do before he was so unfairly done away with?"

"He rang the bells at the monastery."

"And do you want to spend your life ringing bells?"

"Don't make jokes, Mother. You know what I like to do. I like to read and write . . ."

"And dream!" his mother put in.

"You may call it dreaming. I call it thinking."

"Dreaming—thinking. It's a waste of time, whatever you call it. I vow, Thomas, I shall never understand you. Why don't you want to be abbot of Monte Cassino?"

"Well, in the first place . . ."

But Theodora had no intention of letting the boy finish. She interrupted loudly. "Let me tell you, Thomas. I know you. I know that little mind of yours. You probably think the abbot of Monte Cassino has too much power—too much worldly power, that is. You probably think you couldn't be an abbot and a holy man at the same time."

"Oh, no, Mother. The present abbot is a very holy man."

"Well, there you are. Have you any other objections?"

"I'm not cut out to be an abbot!"

"Why not?"

"An abbot runs things. He's an administrator. I'm not good at running things. After all, Mother, God doesn't give all of us the same abilities. He gives us different ones, meaning, I suppose, that he wants each of us to serve him in a different way. It's like—well, as it says in . . ."

The boy faltered. His eyes moved from the path of his mother's gaze. Then, in a new and higher voice, he went on: "The spiritual gifts we have differ according to the special grace which has been assigned to each. If a man is a prophet, let him prophesy. . . . The administrator must be content with his administration, the teacher with his work of teaching, the preacher with his preaching. Each must perform his own task well."

He fell silent, his head bowed before his mother's curious stare. "I must say, Thomas," she said quietly, "for a boy you have an amazing fund of words."

"Those weren't my words, Mother. Those were the words of Saint Paul."

Theodora shrugged. "You may know your Saint Paul, Thomas, but I know the world. And I say this to you—and I say it for the last time. When you return from Naples, you will be abbot of Monte Cassino!"

She crossed the room. Opening the hall door she stood briefly in the opening. "A simple monk!" Her lips trembled. "A son of the Lord of Aquino a simple monk! Never!" Her voice rang out. "Never!" She pulled the door to and was gone.

Thomas, still sitting on the edge of his bed, sighed and stared at his feet. "I wonder", he said in a firm voice, "if Mother will ever understand!"

He looked up, startled by a low chuckle. He had forgotten about Fellow. The young varlet lumbered toward him. "Talking to yourself again, Master Thomas?"

"I guess so." Thomas sighed. "Did you hear what Mother said?"

"Oh, yes." Fellow seated himself on the bed near his master. "So it's off to Naples now, eh?"

"I wasn't referring to that. I mean what I have to do after Naples."

"Oh, that!" With a slap of his big hand Fellow swept "that" away as though it were a fly. "Something tells me, Master Thomas, that after you've finished at Naples, your mother will have nothing to say about what you do. God will tend to that."

"Do you think God will let me be a simple monk?"

A dry, unsmiling chuckle shook the varlet's chest. "We'll see, we'll see. One thing I can tell you. Simple monks do a lot of good. I, myself, owe a great deal to one."

"Who, Fellow?"

"I never knew his name. People called him the white monk."

"White?"

"The color of his habit, Master Thomas. He wore a white robe with a black hood and cloak. He was down here in the village of Rocca Secca at the foot of the hill. He was staying with a peasant family. He had no money. He said he and the other members of his order never did have. They just wander around. They beg for their food and shelter and preach to the people."

"Did he preach in Rocca Secca?"

Fellow nodded. "All the peasants came to hear him and some of the varlets from the castle. It was great preaching, too. Some priests use big words that a man like me can't understand. Not the white monk. There was a lot of us listening to him, but I got the feeling that he was talking just to me. When he'd finished, I understood my religion better. I appreciated it more, too."

"And his order, Fellow? Did the white monk tell you the name of his order?"

"I think he did, but I don't remember. He said it was founded by a man named Dominic."

"Dominic Guzman?"

Fellow cast a sharp look at the boy. "Trust you to know all about it, Master Thomas."

"But I don't. I've heard the name, that's all. I know Dominic founded an order, and I think he was from Spain."

"Yes, from Spain. The white monk told us that. But as to the name of his order . . ." Fellow shook his head. "It runs in my mind that the word 'preachers' was in it. Friars Preachers, maybe, or Begging Preachers, or maybe it was Preaching Beggars. But there, Master Thomas, you can inquire when you get to Naples." Fellow grinned suddenly and lowered his right eye in a wink. "Maybe after you've found out the name of the white monk's order, you'll look into it, Master Thomas."

The boy was grinning, too. "Maybe I will", he said, returning the wink.

7

GOD'S OTHER LANTERN

THE DARKNESS of a mild spring evening in the year
1243 was lowering over the great city of Naples. A
fresh breeze, coming off the bay, rolled up one of the
main streets—a long street called the Via Mazzocannone.
All along the busy, tunnel-like thoroughfare the colored
lanterns in front of the lodging houses were being

lighted. They dropped a splash of red here, a garish stream of yellow there.

The street was so narrow and ran between buildings so tall and so thickly set that the noise of the crowds had no place to go. It hovered, an endless murmur, in the air. Fronting every floor of every building was a balcony. The people sitting on one balcony chatted easily with their neighbors on the balcony across the way.

Down below, on the cobblestone pavement, raggedly dressed children played among the passersby. Beggars wailed their piteous song: "Alms for the love of God! Alms in the name of Christ!"

Thomas Aquinas walked slowly up the street. At eighteen, Thomas had arrived at his full height. Over six feet tall and very heavy, he had become a great slab of a man. His frame had widened over the years, and he bore his tremendous weight with dignity and with ease.

During his four years at the University of Naples, Thomas had strolled the Via Mazzocannone a thousand times. But he never tired of its ever-changing sights and sounds. God had given Thomas a curious and inquiring mind; and to the curious and inquiring, the everlasting variety of God's world is a source of constant joy.

As he walked along, the delicate strains of a lute and the click of castanets reached his ears. He quickened his pace slightly. A block or so farther on, near a large fountain, he found a crowd of people listening to a small troupe of jongleurs, as the wandering entertainers of the Middle Ages were called.

Standing on the stone steps of the fountain in their brightly colored garments, the jongleurs were singing a popular ballad of the day. Thomas smiled to himself as the familiar words floated down:

> Oh! how sweet the breeze of April,
>   Breathing soft as May draws near!
> While, through nights of tranquil beauty,
>   Songs of gladness meet the ear:
> Every bird his well-known language
>   Uttering in the morning's pride,
>   Revelling in joy and gladness
> By his happy partner's side.

Thomas walked on. His destination was a church farther up the street—a church called San Domenico Maggiore. As he mounted the steps leading to the church courtyard, Thomas thought fondly of his varlet, Fellow. It was Fellow who had first told him about the white monks. In Naples, San Domenico Maggiore was their church, for the white monks were the Dominicans, officially known as the Order of Preachers (O.P.).

The glow of candles flickered over the pavement of the court. It came from the votive lights at the base of a tall crucifix against the street wall. Inside the church a number of people were kneeling or standing about in the spacious room. There were no seats.

Thomas said his prayers. Then he walked into a small chapel to one side. As he entered the chapel, a smile creased his lips. Standing on the steps before the little altar, speaking to a group of young men, was his favorite among the Dominican preachers, Brother John of Saint Julian.

Brother John of Saint Julian was an old man, thin and frail. Like the other members of the Order of Preachers, he had spent much of his life begging his way through the countryside, preaching to the poor. Hardship had sharpened his features, but long living in the out-of-doors had left its mark too. His old eyes were clear. There was still color in his sunken cheeks.

He noticed Thomas coming in. He stopped whatever he had been saying and nodded to him above the heads of the others. "Good evening, Thomas", he said. "It's good to see you."

"It is good to be here, Brother John", Thomas replied. "Please go on. I came to listen."

Brother John went on with his talk. "As I was remarking," he said, "we stand today on the threshold of a new and, let us hope, better era. Everywhere men are beginning to realize that God gave us our minds to use. God wants us to study and to learn. It pleases him, I am sure, to see so many great centers of learning—so many universities—springing up all over the Christian world."

A hand rose among the young men listening to Brother John. The old Dominican inclined his head toward the youth who had lifted it. "Yes, my son," he said, "you have a question to ask?"

The young man had a pleasant, resonant voice. "I do,

Brother John", he replied. "A short while ago my mother came to visit me here in Naples. We are a poor family. It was the first time my old mother had ever traveled beyond the boundaries of our little mountain village. She visited some of my classes with me and was shocked by what she heard."

"I am sorry to hear that, my son. What shocked your good mother?"

"The fact, Brother John, that I'm getting so much education. Mother thinks if I continue to study and to learn, doubts will rise in my mind. As a result, according to her, I may some day lose my faith."

Brother John was smiling. "Tell me," he said to the young man, "how long have you studied at the university?"

"This is my fourth year."

"Do you feel that you have learned anything?"

"I believe, in all humility, that I have learned a great deal."

"Do you feel that what you have learned has shaken your faith in any way?"

"On the contrary. My faith has become stronger."

"Good!" Brother John's bright eyes snapped. "I hope you told your mother as much. After all, gentlemen, why do we study? Why do we work into the night, poring over huge books? Why do we try to gather to ourselves all the knowledge of God's good world that we possibly can? Why? Why? What are we students looking for? Who would like to answer that question?"

The young man who had spoken before lifted his hand again. "We are looking for the truth", he said.

"And what is the truth, young man?"

"Our Lord answered that question centuries ago. Our Lord said, 'I am the truth.'"

"Exactly!" Brother John's bony hands met in a loud clap. "Exactly!" he repeated with enthusiasm. "All study worthy of the name is a search for truth. Therefore, all study worthy of the name is bound, sooner or later, to lead to God. Oh, I won't say that we students don't get on the wrong path sometimes. Many a good student goes first in one wrong direction and then another. But if he is really looking for the truth, he is certain to come back to God in the end. Why? Because, as our Lord told us, God is truth and truth is God!"

Brother John lifted one of his arms so that the folds of his white sleeve trembled in the air. "My friends," he said, "God has given each of us two lanterns to guide our steps. One is the lantern of faith. The other is the lantern of reason. Faith is the greatest of all God's gifts to us. God has revealed to us many truths about himself. We do not fully understand these revealed truths, but we accept them. We accept them because the light of faith shows us that they come from God. Reason is simply another word for understanding—understanding of God's will, understanding of ourselves and understanding of the world in which we live. We increase this understanding by studying and learning and thinking."

The old man smiled again at his listeners. "One thing

you must keep in mind", he told them. "A person can find his way to heaven in the light of faith alone. But his path becomes all the brighter when he makes use, also, of God's other lantern—when he travels in the light of both faith and reason."

Brother John of Saint Julian lowered his arm. "Now," he said, "are there any other questions?" None came, so he went on. "Then I'll end this lecture now. However, I will be here as usual tomorrow evening. Any or all of you will be welcome."

The students parted to let the old Dominican come through the chapel. He stopped as he reached Thomas. "I hear", he said, taking Thomas' hand, "that you still plan to become a member of our order."

Thomas nodded. "Yes, Brother John. I expect soon to take the habit of the Dominicans."

The old man released Thomas' hand and left the chapel rapidly. Thomas moved along with the other students. Minutes later, leaving the church itself, he caught another glimpse of the old Dominican. Brother John was gliding across the front courtyard in the direction of the monastery next door.

At almost the same moment Thomas noticed a slender young man leaning against the outer courtyard wall near the monastery. In the moving light of the votive lights there was something about the young man, something familiar . . .

Thomas gasped suddenly and batted his eyes. He found it hard to believe that what he saw was actually

taking place. The young man slowly lifted his head toward the sky. At the same time he extended his right
foot.

Brother John, hastening along, had eyes only for the
monastery door. Before Thomas could cry out, Brother
John had tripped over the extended foot.

Thomas broke into a run. Concern surged in him,
concern for the old man and anger at the younger one.
He could see the young man now, bending over the
fallen monk. He could hear him speaking, his voice oily
with pretended sympathy. It was a spun-out, irritating
drawl of a voice.

Brother John was on his feet when Thomas arrived.
"I'm all right, quite all right", he was saying. He brushed
the dust from his habit. "A few bruises maybe, but no
bones broken, I assure you."

Thomas glared at the other man. "So it's you!" he
exclaimed. "What are you doing here?"

"Waiting for you, of course, Thomas. A good thing,
too. If I hadn't been here, who would have given this
poor old man a hand?"

Brother John was looking from face to face. "I take
it", he said, "that you know one another."

"Yes", Thomas informed him. "This is my brother,
Sir Ronald. Brother John of Saint Julian, Ronald."

Ronald grabbed and pumped the old monk's hand
ferociously. "It's a privilege to meet you, Brother John."
He lowered his eyes, looking about with exaggerated
interest. "There must be something wrong with the

courtyard here. Perhaps one of the paving blocks is loose."

"There is nothing wrong with the paving, Ronald", Thomas said sharply. He turned to Brother John. "Are you sure you're all right? Suppose I walk with you as far as your cell."

"No, no, Thomas. This old frame has seen its best days, but it will carry me down the monastery hall. Besides, you two want to be alone. You must have a great deal to say to one another." He gave each of the brothers a nod. "My respects to you again, Sir Ronald. As for you, Thomas, I expect I will see you tomorrow evening."

"If not sooner, Brother John!"

Thomas waited until the old monk was inside the monastery before turning to Ronald. "I suppose", he said, "that you're very proud of yourself."

"Whatever do you mean, brother dear?" Ronald, elegantly dressed as always, flicked a non-existent spot from the slashed sleeve of his doublet. He flicked another, equally imaginary, from the gaudy black and yellow of his trunks.

"I saw you put your foot out, Ronald. Why did you do it? What have you got against the old man?"

"He's a Dominican, isn't he?"

"You know he is."

"That's why I tripped him. That's how I feel about all Dominicans."

"What do you know about them?"

"What is there to know? They and that other mendi-cant order, the Franciscans! Upstarts, both of them. Who had so much as heard of either order twenty years ago, or, at any rate, fifty? Who of the least importance cares about them now? They're a disgrace to the Church, both of them."

"And I say, Ronald, that they're a blessing to the Church. The Dominicans and the Franciscans carry the word of God to the common people. Thousands of the poor would be lost to the Church if it weren't for those two orders."

"Nonsense! If the poor people want to hear the word of God, let them listen to a decently dressed priest. Your Dominicans and your Franciscans run around the coun-tryside like wild men, begging their way like tramps. Yes, and they look and smell like tramps, too. Ugh! The very thought of them makes me itch."

Ronald took a handkerchief from his doublet sleeve. He carried it to his nostrils in a manner so like his mother that, angry as he was, Thomas had trouble hid-ing a laugh. "May I remind you, Ronald," he said, "that our Lord and his apostles did not travel in style?"

"That was a long time ago. The Church was young then, and poor. It's old now, and rich. But enough of this. I bring a message to you from our noble mother. She says you are not to join the Dominicans."

"She has already said as much in her letters."

"I know. But she is not satisfied with the letters you have written in return. She asked me to come and speak to you personally. You know our mother, Thomas. Now that our noble father is dead, God rest his soul, she is more concerned than ever about the future of her children."

"I'm sure she is." Thomas spoke a little sharply and with a slight smile.

Ronald chuckled. "Nothing is changed, Thomas, so far as Mother is concerned. When you have finished here, you are to return to Monte Cassino."

"As abbot?"

Ronald nodded. "I wouldn't put you in charge of the least of my hunting hawks. I feel sorry for the Benedictines. Their poor old order will probably crumble to ruin when you take over. But Lady Theodora says abbot—so abbot it will be. And now, if you don't mind, I will go and have a drink—alone!"

"One minute, Brother."

Ronald had reached the steps leading down from the courtyard to the street. He turned, facing his brother again. The light from the votive lamps under the crucifix brought out the sheen of his black boots. "Yes?" he said impatiently.

"Do you see Mother often, Ronald?"

"I'm with the emperor, of course. However, I get to Rocca Secca now and then. Do you have a message for her?"

"Yes. Remind her, please, that I'm eighteen now. I no longer have to have her permission for what I do."

Ronald returned to his brother. He stood before him,

his hands on his hips. "Don't be a fool", he drawled. "You can join the preaching beggars five times over. Five times your mother will pull you out of them. She will drag you to Monte Cassino. Yes, she will throw you onto the abbot's throne if she has to use every soldier in her command to do it. Good night, Thomas!"

"Good night, Ronald."

Thomas watched his brother go down the steps and disappear among the noisy street crowds. He stood for quite a while, staring at nothing. Then, turning around, he walked slowly into the monastery and down the hall to the cell of Brother John of Saint Julian.

Early the next morning, in the Dominican priory of Naples—as the monastery next to the church of San Domenico Maggiore was properly called—a solemn ceremony took place. It was the ceremony by which a young man enters the religious life as a novice.

The ceremony took place in the chapter room, the high-ceilinged meeting room of the Dominicans. The first light of dawn purpled the tall, slit windows as the prior—the superior of the priory—entered the room and seated himself in a chair on a raised platform at one end. After that, all the other friars of the priory came in and stood in two rows on either side of the room.

Last of all Thomas Aquinas came in. He wore no outer garments—only the long, black trunks he usually wore under his street clothes and a white shirt that had neither collar nor cuffs. He stood in the center of the room, facing Father Prior.

For a few minutes all heads bowed in silent prayer. Looking up again, Thomas' eyes rested briefly on those of Brother John of Saint Julian, who was standing among the other friars. There was a subdued smile on the old man's lips.

Then the novice master stepped forward. At a signal from him, Thomas prostrated himself, face downward, on the floor. He stretched out his arms so that his body took the form of a cross.

Father Prior spoke.

"Thomas Aquinas," he said, "what do you seek?"

Thomas' voice was muffled by the closeness of his mouth to the stone floor. "The mercy of God and yours", he answered.

"Thomas," the prior continued, "can you tell me the device—that is, the motto and watchword—of the Dominicans?"

"The device of the Dominicans is *Veritas*, meaning truth."

"And what was it, Thomas, that our saintly founder said to his sons?"

"Dominic, the saintly founder of the Dominicans, said, 'Seek the truth in work and in prayer, spread it by word of mouth and by the example of a holy life.'"

Another signal from the novice master and Thomas rose and walked up to the platform. He knelt there at the feet of Father Prior.

"Thomas," Father Prior said, "I must now say certain things to you. Some of these matters we have discussed before. I repeat them here so that there will be no misunderstanding. Are you quite ready to hear what I have to say?"

"I am ready."

A smile flickered briefly over Father Prior's seamed face. "Now then," he said, "when you have taken the habit, you will become a novice for one year. During that year you must search your conscience carefully. If you find that the life of a Dominican friar of the Order of Preachers is not truly your vocation, then you must leave the order. If you find that it is, then, at the end of the year, you must take the vows of poverty, chastity, and obedience, after which you will become a fully professed Dominican. Now then, Thomas, is all that I have said so far clear to you?"

"It is clear."

"Good. I will proceed to another matter. Yours is a special case. Our original plan was to let you take the habit at a much later date, thus giving you more time to think things over. Then last night you received a message from your mother. You passed that message on to Brother John of Saint Julian. On his advice, we are holding the ceremony now. Is all of this in accordance with your understanding?"

"It is."

Father Prior smiled again. "Ordinarily," he said, "this ceremony is held in the church. The church, however, is a public place, so we have held it here, in private, in secret. Our hope is that your family will not hear of it—at least for the time being. However, we can take no chances. Later today you will set out for Rome. When you arrive in Rome you will go to the Dominican house. By then we will know what your family is going to do. If they make no attempt to take you from us, you will probably remain in Rome. If they do—then you will have to leave the country. You will have to go to France, where you will be beyond their reach."

Thomas had lifted his head slightly. "You wished to say something?" Father Prior asked him.

"Yes, Father Prior. King Louis the Ninth of France is a relative of my family. My mother might persuade him to have me sent home."

Father Prior shook his head, smiling. "The saintly Louis the Ninth", he said, "is one of the best friends we Dominicans have. He would not permit your mother to remove you from the order."

"I am glad to hear that, Father Prior."

"Now then, Thomas—I will put to you the big question. I beg of you, let your heart answer. Once you have taken the habit you must obey your superiors in all things. Are you willing to do so?"

"I am, Father Prior."

As the friars sang *Veni, Creator Spiritus*—"Come, Holy Spirit"—the ceremony continued. Thomas was dressed in a habit by Father Prior, assisted by the novice master and a lay brother. First the long white robe was placed on him, then the leather belt with the rosary beads hanging from the left side. Next the scapular, a long white strip of wool, was draped over his shoulders so that it hung down in front and in back. Then the white capuche—that is, the cowl—of his habit was spread across his shoulders and the hood of it was placed on the tip of his head. Finally came the black cappa—the cloak—and still another cowl, a black one.

Thomas stood up dressed as a Dominican friar. Then, as the members of the community sang the beautiful hymn of praise *Te Deum*, Thomas passed among his Dominican brothers to receive the kiss of peace.

Father Prior turned his head slightly. "Brother Robert", he called.

One of the younger friars ascended the low platform and stood beside Thomas. Brother Robert was as tall as Thomas, but he was all skin and bones. The circle of hair around his bald spot, his tonsure, was the color of cornsilk. He had dancing blue eyes in a bony, pinched, pleasant face.

"I am at your service, Father Prior", he said.

Father Prior was still smiling. "Brother Robert," he said, "I place this novice in your hands. It is you who will go with him to Rome—to France too, if that be necessary."

"I will guard him to the best of my ability", Brother Robert said.

"Good. Kneel, then."

They knelt—the tall and skinny young friar and the

tall and thickly set young novice. With a solemn sweep of his hand, Father Prior gave them his blessing in the name of the Father and of the Son and of the Holy Spirit.

8

KIDNAPPED!

A RUST-COLORED CLOUD scudded across the evening sky above the little village of Acquapendente, some forty miles north of Rome. On the single rutted lane between the low, thatched houses, knots of people gathered. They were talking in excited tones of the event that had suddenly quickened their quiet lives.

Early that morning two knights in gleaming armor had ridden into the village, followed by a small party of soldiers and armed varlets. The knights said they were looking for their young brother. They described him as a tall, heavy-set youth, dressed in the habit of a Dominican friar and probably accompanied by an older member of his order.

All morning the knights and their men had remained in the village. They had gone from one fenced-in cottage to another. They had lifted the latch on every oaken door and poked around the single, soot-blackened room of every dwelling place. They had searched some of the hay mows and at least half of the cow sheds. Finally, shortly after noon, they had ridden on, taking the northern road in the direction of Florence.

And now the villagers were reliving the strange event. Now they talked. And now, in the dark corner of a cow shed behind the largest of the village cottages, Thomas Aquinas awakened from a long, sound sleep.

He awakened slowly and stared into the sagging web a spider had drawn between the dusty rafters above. He sat up and looked around. Brother Robert, long since awake and leaning against the wooden wall, grinned at him and closed one of his dancing blue eyes.

"Well, Thomas," he said, "do you feel better now?"

"Much better, Brother Robert."

"And your feet?"

Thomas bent forward. His feet were bare. He sighed as he examined them.

"Still some blisters, I'm afraid", he said.

Thomas had earned those blisters. It had taken Thomas and Brother Robert a week to walk the 150 miles from Naples to Rome. In Rome the worst possible news awaited them. Lady Theodora knew what had happened. She had summoned her sons Landulph and Ronald to the castle. She had ordered them to take a body of armed men and search for Thomas. She had told them to find Thomas and take him away from those "nasty beggars" if they had to ride to the ends of the earth to do it.

Thomas and Brother Robert had remained less than a day in Rome. Since leaving the imperial city, they had been on the road for almost four days. They had traveled only by night. As they stumbled into the village late the night before, Thomas' feet had given out. A peasant and his family took them in. When Thomas' brothers were sighted in the early morning, the peasant hid them in his cowshed.

Thomas sighed again. Getting up and leaning one hand against the wall, he started to pull on his white leg-coverings. "I must have fallen asleep the minute we got here", he said. "Did my brothers and their party search the shed?"

"No." Brother Robert shook his head. "I heard them for a while in the farmyard. Then the little boy, the peasant's son, told them a white lie. He said he *thought* he had seen two friars elsewhere in the village. To my surprise and relief they believed him. Incidentally, Thomas, which is which?"

"Which is which what?"

"Your brothers? Which is the big one—the one who looks like you?"

"That's Landulph. He's a fine man, really—all bark and no bite, if you know what I mean. The other one's Ronald."

"And who is Fellow?"

"Fellow!" Thomas stopped what he was doing. "Fellow!" he exclaimed. "Was Fellow with them?"

"Your brothers kept talking to a varlet they called Fellow."

"My personal varlet, Brother Robert. He's the person who first told me about the Dominicans. If Fellow's with them, he'll do everything he can to see that they don't catch us."

The door of the cowshed squeaked open and a small boy, the peasant's son, stepped in. He carried a lighted lantern. He was a sturdy lad with a thin, high-cheekboned face and velvety black eyes.

"I heard you talking, fathers," he said, "so I knew you were awake."

Brother Robert had risen. "We're not fathers, boy. Brother Thomas." He nodded at Thomas. "And I am Brother Robert."

"You're men of God", the boy said simply. "Naught else matters with me." He turned to Thomas. "Papa says your brothers have made their camp for the night at the pass."

"The pass?"

"It's a few miles north of us here. The road goes between two steep hills. Papa says I'm to hide you in some hay on the cart and carry you past the camp that way. He says he's sure we can make it in the darkness."

Brother Robert frowned. "What if they stop the cart and search it?" he asked.

"It'll be very dark in the pass when we get there, Brother Robert. They may not even see us."

Brother Robert shook his head, unsatisfied. "Is there no other way? Could we not walk around the pass?"

"You could." The boy shrugged his thin shoulders. "But it would take days. And seeing how it is with Brother Thomas' feet . . ."

Brother Robert nodded.

Out in the farmyard the boy had already hitched a donkey to a two-wheeled cart piled high with hay. For a time Thomas and Brother Robert sat atop the hay. As they jogged out of town and northward, the last of the evening light drained from the cloudy sky. Darkness took over. There were only a few stars, Thomas noted, and only the beginnings of a moon.

They had not gone far when the boy stopped the cart. "The pass is at the foot of the next hill", he told them. He leaped to the road. Thomas and Brother Robert burrowed as deeply as they could into the hay. Then the peasant boy saw to it that they were properly covered.

Resuming his place on the cart, he urged the old donkey on. It was a cool night, but little of the cool air reached Thomas deep under the rancid-smelling hay. A piece of it tickled his nostrils. To keep from sneezing, he pressed one of his hands against his upper lip.

He could hear Brother Robert muttering nearby. "Don't move if you can help it, Thomas. Keep as still as you can."

He left his hand where it was. As the dark seconds passed and seemed to become years, his unnatural position became painfully uncomfortable. Breathing became harder and harder.

Then, suddenly, he had other things to worry about. Voices. Voices coming rapidly nearer! And along with the voices, the beat of horses' hoofs!

The peasant boy had explained on the way out that Landulph and Ronald might make their camp on the level ground high on one of the hills. With the camp so far up, there was a good chance they could slip through the pass unnoticed.

Obviously this was not to be! The voices were all around now—the voices and the clatter. Thomas could hear the heavy breathing of the horses. His ears picked out Ronald's spun-out drawl, his brother Landulph's loose bass. They were talking to the peasant boy, he could tell. He made a futile effort to hear the lighter voice of the lad as he answered.

Then he heard Fellow's shout—very loud, very close at hand. "Did I hear you say the hay should be searched, Sir Landulph? A good idea. I'll see to it myself."

In spite of his discomfort, Thomas felt like laughing.

That was quick thinking on Fellow's part. Quick thinking, indeed, to suggest that he himself do the searching.

He felt a jiggle in the hay above his head. In the speckled blackness he could make out Fellow's big hand. Apparently the varlet had no sword with him. Or, if he had, he was taking no chances. He was not using it. The hand withdrew and shot in again, closer this time to Thomas' head.

In a sudden, impulsive movement, Thomas wrapped his own hand around Fellow's and gave it a hard, firm squeeze! He let go. He held his breath and then released it. Fellow had returned his squeeze! Fellow understood!

He felt the hay jiggle at other points as the big varlet went all around the cart. "Well, Sir Landulph," he heard him shout finally, "there's a lot of hay on this cart."

"Just hay, Fellow?"

"You heard me, Sir Landulph. There's a lot of hay here."

For a frightened second Thomas was afraid he was going to have to laugh. Fellow had told only the simple truth. There *was* a lot of hay on that cart!

Landulph was shouting now. "All right, then. Back to camp, all of you. We'll post a watch through the night."

The cart was moving again. It shook and bumped over the rough road. Underneath the hay, the rancid fumes grew thicker by the minute. Thomas was beginning to wonder how long he could stand them when he heard the soft voice of the peasant boy. "It's safe now, brothers. You can come out."

He sat up like a shot, gulping in a mouthful of fresh air and flying hay. The boy had stopped the cart. "It will be all right for you to go on by yourselves now, brothers." The boy had turned to the friars. His wide grin was like a light in the gloom.

Brother Robert was already in the road, dusting the hay from his habit. "My boy," he said, "may God bless you for what you have done for us."

Thomas lowered himself slowly from the cart. "What about you, now?" he asked the boy. "When you return through the pass, won't my brothers and their men stop you again? Won't they wonder what has brought you back and maybe hold you till they find out?"

The boy shook his head. "I'll spend the night in one of these gullies", he said. "I won't go back until I see your brothers and their party go by in the morning. You'd better make haste now. The more distance you can cover before dawn, the better."

Thomas and Brother Robert trudged down the road. Some fifty feet away, Thomas halted and turned back. The peasant boy, his cart still standing where he had stopped it, saw him turn and waved. Thomas waved back. Then he hastened to catch up with Brother Robert.

Brother Robert moved with the ease and grace of a cat. He had been a friar for years. Years of tramping the countryside had hardened his lean body. It was otherwise with Thomas. His feet were still a mass of blisters. Every step was an effort.

To take his mind off the pain, he started a conversation. "Tell me, Brother Robert," he said, "if we weren't running away, if we were back in the priory at Naples, what would we be doing now?"

Brother Robert's eyes shot upward to the dark, clouded sky. "We'd be sleeping now, Thomas. But not for long. Come midnight, we'd go to the chapel with the other friars to chant the Divine Office."

"And after that?"

"Another rest. Then we'd rise early in the morning to chant some more of the Office and to attend Mass."

A short distance ahead of them a clump of cypress trees took shape against the night. Thomas could make out the outlines of a stone fountain in their midst.

"And hymns, Brother Robert?" he inquired. "Do the Dominicans sing many hymns?"

"Oh, yes, Thomas. We . . ." Brother Robert ceased walking suddenly, a cry of dismay on his lips.

Thomas had stumbled. He would have fallen had not Brother Robert hastened to his side. "I'm sorry!" he cried. "I'm going much too fast. I keep forgetting that you're not used to so much walking."

"It's I who should be sorry, Brother Robert. I'm ashamed of myself."

"No need to be. I was a friar many years before my feet got hardened." Brother Robert, too, had noticed the fountain. He guided Thomas over and ordered him to remove his leggings and soak his tortured feet.

The water was chilly, but soothing. For some time

Thomas sat on the stone rim. Stepping out, he smiled to himself. Brother Robert had thrown himself on the grass. Thomas could tell by the friar's deep breathing that he had gone to sleep.

"Poor Brother Robert!" Thomas thought. Quite likely the lean friar had not gotten as much sleep during the day as he had.

He sat down and leaned against the fountain wall. He would sit there, he decided, until his feet dried—maybe a little longer—so that Brother Robert could get some more rest. He would have to awaken him soon, of course, because . . . because . . .

The thought never completed itself. With a sudden jerk his head dropped forward and he himself slept.

A dream came to him. Brother Robert's mention of the Divine Office had left its impression on his tired mind. Thomas dreamed that he was back in Monte Cassino. He was in the choir stalls chanting with the Benedictines, chanting:

> The law of the Lord is perfect,
> The fear of the Lord is holy,
> Praise the Lord because he is good,
> Praise the God of Heaven.

Then the dream began to get all mixed up, the way dreams do. He dreamed that he was a child again, only three years old. He dreamed that it was night and that he was in his bedroom at the castle of Rocca Secca. He was not alone. In a crib by the bed lay his baby sister, her nurse dozing on a nearby chair.

It was storming outside. Thunder crashed and boomed through the castle courtyards. Suddenly there was a blinding flash of lightning. The night at the windows turned to day, and a great sheet of light flapped through the room. He saw the nurse rise. He saw the door open, and his mother came in, carrying a candle. She hurried to the crib. He could hear her screaming, "She's dead— my little girl is dead! Oh, my God, my God!"

What strange words his mother was using. "Mother!" His own voice mingled with her sobs. "Mother!" he cried. "What is God? What is God?"

Then he dreamed of another event of his faraway childhood. He dreamed that he was with his mother in Naples, at the public baths. He saw a piece of paper on the tiled floor. He picked it up. There were words on the paper. He could not read yet, but for some reason the words pleased him. He was furious when his mother tore the paper from his hands, saying, "No, no, Thomas; that paper is dirty." Then his mother glanced at the paper. Her eyes softened.

"Mother!" He tugged at her silken pelisse. "What does the paper say?"

His mother read him the words. They were the lovely words of the *Hail Mary*!

After that, he and his mother went out onto the street. There were people all around them. He was still very small. All he could see was the people's legs. . . . But no! Those weren't just people all around him! Those were . . . !

Thomas had awakened. At first he was not sure whether he had or not. He was not sure for a second whether he was awake or still dreaming. Then suddenly things were clear.

Those were horses standing all around him. Daylight had come. He could see the glint of the sun on the horses' silvered trappings. His back still leaned against the wall of the roadside fountain. Brother Robert still slept in the grass beside him.

And the horses all around him bore armored soldiers and armed varlets!

He turned his head slightly. Now his view of the horses was partly blocked by two tall knights standing over him. He looked up with a gasp—and stared into the grinning faces of his brothers.

"Well, now, young runaway!" Ronald's drawl, always irritating to Thomas, was more irritating then ever. "You may not know it, but you are about to be kidnapped by your own kith and kin. You are about to be taken out of the Dominican order and carried to the arms of your anxious mother!"

Thomas neither spoke nor moved. He saw the grin leave his other brother's lips. A frown replaced it. "No nonsense, please, Ronald!" Landulph growled. "Thomas doesn't find this situation funny. To be honest, neither do I." He lowered one of his hands. "Up with you, now."

Thomas did not take the hand. He saw Brother Robert open his blue eyes. He winced as he saw the lean friar take in the situation with a sad and startled look. "It's all my fault, Brother Robert", he said in a low voice. "I meant to awaken you. But then I guess I fell asleep myself."

He was aware that Ronald had bent over and had seized him roughly under one arm. "You heard your brother!" he snarled. "Up with you!"

On his feet, Thomas could see better the faces of the horsemen all around him. He saw Fellow gazing at him. He lowered his eyes. Never had he seen a more unhappy expression on his varlet's face.

Landulph had walked across the clearing. He returned at once, leading a magnificent chestnut palfrey. "Allegro, Thomas!" he cried. "Do you recognize him?"

Thomas gave no sign that he did. He did, of course. Allegro was one of the finest and fastest riding horses in the Rocca Secca stables. "Allegro will get you home all right, my boy", Landulph shouted at him.

Ronald had joined his brother. He whispered something in his ear.

Landulph shook his head angrily. "No, no, Ronald! What difference does it make what he's wearing?"

"It makes a difference to me", Ronald yelled at him. "And I don't have to tell you, it will make a difference to his mother!"

He returned to Thomas, a sneer twisting his thin mouth. "Take off that habit, Thomas!" he ordered. "Take it off at once!"

Thomas stared at him, motionless.

"Do you hear me, Thomas?" Ronald screamed. "Take off that Dominican habit this minute. Take it off, I said! All right, then! I'm going to count to five. Either you take off that beggar's outfit yourself, or I'll tear it off with my own hands."

He counted, "One . . . two . . . !"

With each count anger rose in Thomas, anger such as he had never experienced before. Out of the side of his eye he could see that Brother Robert had gotten to his feet. The tall friar was shaking his head at him as though he had already guessed what Thomas was about to do.

"Five!" Ronald roared. He reached out, seizing a handful of Thomas' woolen habit.

There was a loud, tearing sound. Only one! A memory flashed into Thomas mind. He remembered a classroom at the University of Naples. He remembered something one of his favorite teachers had done to a student who had refused to behave himself. His left arm shot forward. Two of his strong fingers clamped onto Ronald's skinny nose! At the same moment, his right hand swooped through the air and slapped Ronald's cheek with the force of a sledge hammer!

Ronald would have fallen if Thomas' fingers, still clamping his nose, had not held him, swaying, on his feet.

Thomas withdrew his hand and closed his eyes. All anger left him. A prayer lifted itself to his lips. "Forgive me, God. Forgive me!" He heard a low chuckle, then a louder one. When he opened his eyes, he saw that Landulph was bent double with laughter. So were most of the soldiers and varlets.

Ronald's face was white with rage. He made no effort, however, to attack Thomas again. Landulph brought the chestnut riding horse over. He pushed Ronald roughly aside and shouted at Thomas.

"All right, my boy. Onto your horse now. We've wasted enough time here."

Thomas did not budge. He felt Brother Robert's hand on his arm. "Do as he says, Thomas", Brother Robert murmured. "They are going to take you anyhow."

Thomas gave the lean friar a sad smile; but that was his only movement.

"Please, Thomas. Onto the horse!" Landulph's deep voice was trembling now, as though he were on the verge of tears. "Please, Thomas. Don't make us use force!"

"I have no desire to go with you, Landulph", Thomas said quietly. "If you want me on that horse, put me there."

"May the saints preserve us!" Landulph whirled away from his brother. "You, you!" He pointed to two of the varlets. "Put this boy on his horse!"

Thomas did not resist the varlets. Neither did he co-operate with them. When they lifted him, they found themselves with a dead weight in their arms, a very statue of a man. At a barked order from Landulph, two more varlets came to their assistance. Together, they managed to put Thomas on the horse. They were unable, however, to sit him up. The best they could was to throw him over the chestnut palfrey, face downward, like a sack of meal.

Thomas was no sooner in this position than he realized that Fellow had dismounted and was standing beside him. "Please, Master Thomas", Fellow whispered. "We have a long journey ahead to Rocca Secca. You might as well be comfortable."

With his head dangling in midair, Thomas smiled at his varlet. "You knew I was hiding on the cart back there, didn't you, Fellow?" He, too, was whispering.

Fellow nodded and grinned. "Please, Master Thomas. Sit up."

With Fellow's help, Thomas righted himself. The horsemen had formed two long lines on either side of him. Up ahead Landulph bellowed the order to march.

A brilliant morning had succeeded the cloudy night. For a long while Thomas rode looking backward over his shoulder. He jogged along in this manner until the column of men and horses rounded a corner and the white-clad figure of Brother Robert, standing against the fountain, disappeared from view.

9

THE PRISONER IN THE TOWER

IN THE ORANGE GLOW of a spring dawn five days later,
the column of horses and men led by Landulph and
Ronald galloped across the field and across the lowered
drawbridge into the castle of Rocca Secca.

The fast journey had left Thomas aching in every
bone and muscle. The stir within the castle walls made

little or no impression. A varlet helped him off his horse. Then, flanked by his brothers, he walked across the inner court and through a vestibule into the great hall of his family's palace.

The servants had recently scattered new rushes over the stone floor. They brought the pleasing fragrance of the out-of-doors into the huge, vault-like room. Low flames, playing along the tree trunks in the fireplace, cast a fitful pattern of light and shade.

On a low platform near one of the windows, Lady Theodora bent over a large needlework frame. Her morning routine was always the same. Rising at first light, she dressed with the help of her maids and attended Mass at the castle chapel. Then came a light breakfast, after which she spent the next two hours at her needlework.

On the window bench behind her sat two attractive young ladies—the younger of Thomas' three sisters. They and their mother looked up as the men trooped in, bowing and hastily removing their headgear. While the other members of the party clustered about the door, Thomas and his brothers advanced to the foot of the platform.

Thomas felt Landulph's arm slip around his shoulders. "Well, Mother," he heard him saying, "here he is."

Nothing moved in Lady Theodora's large dark eyes. One of her long hands still held the needle with which she was working. "Well done, Landulph", she said. "You, too, Ronald."

She nodded, and Thomas' brothers, leaving his side, joined the other men at the rear of the room.

For some seconds Thomas and his mother regarded one another in silence.

"Oh, Thomas, Thomas." The countess spoke softly. "Have you any idea how much you have hurt your mother?"

She bowed her head suddenly so that Thomas found himself staring into the thick crown of her glossy blue-black hair. "Look at me", she commanded. "A month ago I was a comparatively young woman. But look at me now. Look at the gray in my hair. You have done this to me, Thomas. You have done it!"

She lifted her head and gazed at Thomas. He met her look with one of affection—and slight amusement. His mother, he realized, was play-acting. She was trying to play on his sympathies. Actually, she still looked young—very young—for a mother of nine children, four of whom were already married and living in homes of their own.

"But now, now," she was saying in a still-soft voice, "now you are home; and now we can begin a new life together, can't we? And now. . ." She jabbed her needle into the cloth of silk and gold stretched across her needle-work frame. "And now," she went on, her youthful voice rising and singing out loud and clear, "my question, Thomas. My one question. Are you ready now to remove that horrid beggar's habit and to become abbot of Monte Cassino? Only say yes to that and your poor broken old mother stands ready to forget and forgive everything. Speak up, Thomas! What is your answer— are you ready now to become abbot of Monte Cassino?"

Thomas could feel the silence that filled the big, shadowy room when his mother finished speaking and fell back in her chair.

He glanced at the parted lips of his sister Marotta, sitting on the window bench behind Lady Theodora. Marotta, only a year older than himself, had been a tomboy in her youth. She had grown into a slender young woman of dignity and beauty. She had large dark eyes and freshly colored cheeks.

Thomas somehow got the feeling that Marotta was on his side. He somehow got the feeling that she was hoping he would say . . .

He said it. "No, Mother. I have given my promise to the Dominicans. I will be of their order and wear their habit all the rest of my life. You see, Mother, . . ."

Lady Theodora cut him short with a low moan.

She had risen. She kicked the train of her pelisse to one side and stepped forward. "Take it back, Thomas", she pleaded. "Take back what you have just said. Once more I put my question to you: Are you ready now to leave the Dominicans and become abbot of Monte Cassino?"

Once more Thomas replied, "No, Mother."

She took another step forward. "My son," she cried, "I would not harm you for the world, but you leave me no choice." She raised her eyes, taking in the men clustered about the door at the far end of the hall. "Hear me!" she shouted. "I command that my son Thomas be taken to the top room of the donjon tower. I command that he be imprisoned there until he comes to his senses!"

With a sharply lifted arm she stilled an outburst of murmurs. "I hereby take a solemn vow," she went on, "and I call on all of you to witness it. When I have finished what I now have to say, I shall close my eyes. Never again will I look on my son Thomas. Never will I speak to him until I receive word that he has consented to do as I ask."

Lady Theodora's ringing tones trailed off, leaving a tense silence. She closed her eyes.

There was a hubbub throughout the room. Thomas heard a terse order behind him. It came in the twanging voice of his brother Ronald. Two varlets had seized his arms. They hustled him out of the great hall. His eyes blinked in the morning sunlight as he was hurried across the inner court to a small door in the donjon tower.

He was too large for anyone to walk beside him up the stone steps. The varlets made him go ahead. They prodded him from time to time, their jeers and taunts echoing and re-echoing up the long, winding stair. For Thomas, endless time passed before he heard the gruff voice of a guard issuing a challenge from the topmost landing.

The varlets answered. The guard said something else. Nothing was clear to Thomas at this point, nothing at

all. The guard marched him down a short hall and unlocked an oaken door with a small grille at the top of it.
He shoved him hard so that Thomas fell into the dimly
lit room beyond—fell and spun on the dusty floor.

Some time passed before he could get his breath again.
He lifted himself on his hands and looked around. He
had been in the donjon tower room once, years before.
An unpleasant room, he remembered—and he saw now
that it had grown more so with the years. A low-burning
fire on a hearth threw harsh shadows over the stone walls
and over the thick cobwebs of the corners. There was a
table with a candle on it, a small chair, some straw
bunched on the floor at one point.

There was a window. After a while he got up and
went over to it. The lower casement came even with the
top of his head. Looking up he could see nothing but a
patch of sky—an oblong patch that, even as he watched,
began to take on color in the slowly swelling arc of the
morning sun.

The donjon tower room was to be Thomas' home for
almost eighteen months. In the beginning he spent a
great part of the time on his knees, saying his Rosary on
the big wooden beads of his habit. In the beginning, too,
his only visitor was the guard who came into the cell
twice a day to bring food and fuel for the fire.

Then early one morning, in the hall beyond the oaken
door, Thomas heard the tap-tap of a lighter step in the
pounding wake of the guard's boots. His heart seemed to

stop beating. Could it be his mother? Was it possible that she had repented of her foolish vow?

But it was not his mother. It was his sister Marotta. The pretty young woman dismissed the guard, looked around once, and burst into tears.

"Oh, come now, Marotta", Thomas murmured. "It's not such a bad place."

"It's dreadful! Dreadful!"

Still crying, Marotta permitted him to guide her to the single chair. "Dreadful!" she wailed. "How could Mother bring herself to do this to you? What a stubborn woman she is!"

"And what a stubborn son she has!" As he spoke, Thomas cocked his big head and gave Marotta such a comical look that she went straight from tears into laughter.

"Oh, Thomas," she cried, "I hadn't thought of it that way. All the same, this time Mother is wrong and you are right. Of that I'm sure."

"And I'm sure Mother thinks she is right."

"I suppose so. I suppose she means well." Marotta looked up at her brother, her small hands holding onto the two long braids that she wore, like her mother, on her shoulders. "Thomas," she said, "how old were you when it came to you that Mother wasn't always right about things?"

"I was about fourteen. Why?"

"Did you feel anything?"

"What do you mean, Marotta?"

"The first time I decided Mother was wrong about something, I felt perfectly dreadful. Dreadful! I remember saying to myself, 'How dare you believe that Mother could be wrong about anything!' I felt guilty, Thomas—as if I had committed a murder or something."

"You were growing up."

"Was I?"

Thomas nodded. "Part of growing up is when you realize that your parents are human beings. They can make mistakes like anyone else. Realizing that they can is part of growing up, so long as . . ."

Thomas paused and his sister glanced up again. "So long as what?" she inquired.

"So long as you go on loving your parents in spite of their mistakes."

"Oh, I do love Mother."

"So do I, Marotta."

Marotta smiled. She glanced about the dingy room again. "I must go now, Thomas", she said quietly. "I promised Mother to read to her while she does her needlework. But I'll come back early tomorrow evening. What can I bring you then?"

"Books", Thomas replied.

She brought him a batch of books the next morning and more on succeeding days. She brought him writing parchment, too, and quill pens.

Now Thomas was far from unhappy. He placed his wooden table in the shaft of light falling through the single window. There he sat, reading, writing, thinking.

He studied again the foremost theological textbook of his day, a book called the *Sentences* of Peter Lombard. He read and reread his favorite books from the Bible, the Psalms of David and King Solomon's Song of Songs, sometimes called the Canticle of Canticles. He read a book called *Metaphysics*, by Aristotle. Thomas was fascinated by Aristotle. It interested him that Aristotle had been a pagan. Aristotle had done his writing almost four hundred years before the birth of our Lord. Even so, he was able to figure out that God existed. With no knowledge of revealed religion, the great pagan philosopher had discovered—simply by using his head—that the world was moved and ruled by God's eternal laws.

From time to time Thomas pulled away from his table. Slipping to his knees, he said his Rosary. High in his donjon tower prison he was conscious of a deep, deep silence. He began to feel that in this wonderful silence his words reached God's ears quickly indeed. After a while he fell into the habit, from time to time, of simply sitting back in his chair and talking with God. Thus he sat one late afternoon, saying: "God, I have always wanted time and quiet in which to read and think. Now you have given me both in abundance. I have no complaint."

Marotta was only the first of his visitors. Several times his older sister Theodora called on him. Theodora was a tall, stately young woman. Her manner was stiff and standoffish, but her heart was kind. She brought Thomas blankets for his straw bed and candles for his study table.

One morning Theodora brought and introduced to Thomas the young man she was about to marry, the Count of Marisco. Thomas was pleased with the young man's open face and thoughtful manner. It delighted him that his sister was about to make such an excellent marriage.

And one morning his brothers, Landulph and Ronald, stomped into the dark cell.

Landulph could hardly bring himself to look into the eyes of his imprisoned brother. In his deep voice he ground out a few embarrassed remarks—remarks to the effect that the whole thing was "a shame" and that his mother was making "a great mistake". Suddenly his huge face turned a crimson red and he fled from the cell, slamming the oaken door shut behind him.

Ronald lingered on. He stood near the door, surveying Thomas from a distance. "Well, now," he drawled after a while, "that Dominican habit of yours is getting a little dirty, isn't it?"

Thomas knew what his brother was thinking. Ronald, he knew, was a man to hold a grudge. Ronald still smarted over the fact that on the morning of the kidnapping, Thomas had stopped him from removing his habit.

Thomas prayed for patience. He promised God that never again would he lose his temper and strike a man as he had struck Ronald that morning.

"My habit is getting dirty, Ronald", he answered. "After all, it's the only habit I have."

"So it is. And you know, Brother dear, that I think—

and so does your mother—that it is one too many Dominican habits for any man to have."

Ronald moved a few steps closer. He fingered the hilt of the small dagger he wore in a sheath at his waist.

"You may remember", he went on, "that I tried to take that habit away from you once."

"I remember, Ronald."

"You caught me by surprise then, but that won't happen again. Do you hear me, Brother dear? It won't happen that way again."

Thomas said nothing.

In a sudden movement Ronald covered the space between them. With half a dozen strokes of his dagger he slashed the white habit from Thomas' body so that the tattered pieces fell to the floor around him.

Then Ronald was gone from the cell, and Thomas could hear the guard locking the oaken door behind him.

When Marotta entered the cell the next morning her dark eyes clouded at the sight of her brother. She had brought his breakfast in a small basket, which she placed on the table. "Oh, Thomas!" she murmured, staring at him.

Thomas had picked up the tattered pieces of his habit. He had wrapped them around himself as best he could.

"Ronald?" his sister inquired.

Thomas nodded.

Marotta took Thomas' meal out of the basket, pushing his books aside to make room on the small table.

"Never mind", she said. "Before long you will have two new habits."

"What do you mean, Marotta—I will have two new habits?"

"They are being brought to you from Rome. Do you remember the Count of Marisco?"

"Theodora's future husband? Of course."

"He'll bring them to you. He's in Rome now, Thomas. Before he left, Theodora and I had a talk with him. We got a letter this morning. At our request the count called on your superiors."

"At the Dominican priory in Rome?"

"Yes, Thomas. Now, sit down, please, and eat your meal."

Thomas sat down, but he was quite unable to eat. "Go on, Marotta", he pleaded. "What did the count tell my superiors?"

"Everything. They in turn called on the Holy Father."

Thomas half rose in his chair. "Yes, Marotta—and?"

"The Holy Father sent word that unless you were permitted to rejoin your order soon, he would have to excommunicate the Aquino family—all of us, that is, except yourself."

Thomas was fully on his feet now. "Did you and Theodora tell Mother what the Pope said?"

Marotta nodded.

"And what did Mother say?" Thomas asked.

"She said a very strange thing. She said, 'If Thomas

escapes from the tower, I will do nothing about it.' In other words . . .''

"In other words . . .'' Thomas finished the thought for her. "In other words, Mother is too proud to let me go. On the other hand, if I can escape without her knowing it, she'll do nothing about it.''

"That's right.''

"But how, Marotta?'' Thomas glanced at the thick oaken door of his cell. "How?'' he demanded. "How am I to leave here with a man always on guard at the end of the hall out there? Even if I get past him, there are always guards in the courtyard below.''

"There's the window.''

Thomas walked over to the oblong opening, shaking his head. "Impossible'', he muttered. "The donjon tower rises straight up from the hillside at this point.''

"You're forgetting something. Halfway down the hill, below us here, there's a small shelf of level land.''

"True, but how am I to get down there? I can't *fly*, you know.''

"We'll find a way. We've already talked about it— Theodora and I and Fellow.''

"Fellow? You've talked this over with him?''

"Yes, Thomas. And you know Fellow. He'll figure out something. Now sit down and force yourself to eat. Do, Thomas, and I'll tell you some more good news.''

Thomas seated himself. He poked indifferently at the food before him. "Please continue, Marotta'', he begged.

"Very well. Do you know an old friar called Brother John of Saint Julian?"

"He was my favorite teacher at Naples. Why?"

"He's coming to see you, Thomas."

Brother John made his appearance a week later. He, too, assured Thomas that somehow, some way, he would be gotten out of the tower. He instructed him to be hopeful and to say his prayers. On the verge of taking his leave, the old Dominican seized Thomas' hand and held it a long while, looking into the young man's eyes.

"Thomas," he said at length, "I believe you've learned something during your long imprisonment."

Thomas glanced at the books on his desk. "Well, Brother John," he said, "I have tried to go on with the studies I began at Naples."

The old man was shaking his head. "I don't mean that", he said. "I believe you have learned patience."

Thomas dropped his eyes, blushing slightly.

"It is a great virtue", the old friar went on. "Some of us pray for it all our lives in vain."

Thomas had trouble sleeping that night. Several times, throwing aside his blankets, he left his straw bed and knelt on the stone floor to say his Rosary. Once, going to the window, he stood there breathing in the fresh air of the night and talking with God.

"Dear God," he whispered, "I thank you for the patience you have given me. But in all truth I long now to be free. I long to be rejoined with my brother friars, to begin my real life as a Dominican." He bowed his head, remembering and repeating the words of Christ in the garden, "'Yet not as I will, but as you will.'"

He spent the next day, after Marotta had been and gone, reading and praying as usual. So the next day passed in his donjon tower room, and another and another. Toward the end of the week the Count of Marisco brought him the promised habits. Thomas could not thank the young nobleman enough.

The count told him, too, not to give up hope, that plans were being made. Thomas had to smile as the count, taking his leave, used the very word Brother John of Saint Julian had used. "Patience, Brother Thomas", he said. "Patience now!"

The minute Marotta entered the cell the following morning, Thomas knew that something was up. She dismissed the guard immediately. No sooner was he out of the room than she carried the chair over to the door. She stood on it and peered through the grille. Then, jumping down, she returned quickly to Thomas.

"I wanted to be sure the guard was out of earshot", she explained in a hurried whisper. "I can tell you only one thing. Then we must talk no more about it this morning. It's to happen this evening. At sundown! Be ready!"

Twice, as he was eating his meal, Thomas asked his sister what the plans were. Each time she shook her head, put a finger to her lips, and went on talking, in a loud voice, of other matters.

After she had gone, Thomas sat down to his books.

But for once in his life he found it impossible to concentrate on the written word. He paced his cell, back and forth. For hours he stood by the window, looking out. During his long imprisonment that oblong patch of sky up there had become his clock. He could not see the great round ball of the sun itself. All the same, he knew when it lay halfway down the afternoon sky. He knew to the minute when it finally reached a point level with the western horizon.

The guard brought him his supper. He ate hastily so as to be rid of the man. Then he returned to his window. It was dark now. He could make out a handful of distant stars.

Sundown, Marotta had said. Thomas grew nervous. He paced his cell again. Had something gone wrong? Had the plans, whatever they were, somehow gone awry?

Then all at once he stopped pacing and, for a second or two, he stopped breathing. Lantern light flashed in the hall. He could see it through the grille in the oaken door. He could hear the pound of men's feet, too, and what seemed to be some sort of scuffling noise.

He hurried to the door. Unlike Marotta, he had no need of a chair to see through the barred opening. He could make out nothing clearly at first—only the light of lanterns moving every which way. Then a familiar face leaped out of the shadows. Thomas let out a small shout. It was the first time in eighteen months that he had laid eyes on his old friend and varlet, Fellow!

Fellow carried a huge basket in his hand, and Marotta

was trotting along at his side. Behind them came two stocky men. Thomas had the vague feeling that he had seen those men before; at any rate, there was something familiar about their rough faces. Between them they carried a coil of heavy rope.

Marotta had the key of the cell in her hand. She unlocked the door and let Fellow come in ahead of her. The minute he entered, Fellow put down the basket. He grabbed Thomas in a bear hug of such violence that, strong as he was, Thomas wondered if he would come out of it with all his bones unbroken.

"What happened?" he asked when the varlet released him and he could breathe again. "I mean—the scuffle in the hall?"

"Nothing, Master Thomas. The guard met with an accident."

"He isn't dead?"

"A little bump on his head. He'll come out of it in an hour or so and never know what hit him. Now meet two of my big brothers—two of the stoutest men ever to grow up in the village of Rocca Secca."

So that was why the two men with Fellow looked so familiar. They resembled him. They were his brothers. Thomas nodded to them and murmured, "How kind of you to help." He turned to Fellow. "They are stout chaps", he said.

"They're nothing!" Fellow laughed. "You should see our other brother. He could knock our three heads together with one hand tied behind his back. All right, you two!" He gestured at the men behind him. "You know what to do." At once one of the men played out a sizable length of the rope. The other carried the coil itself into the hall. He placed it on the floor so that the remainder of the rope could be guided around the big pillar in the center of the tower.

Marotta was tugging at Thomas' sleeve. "As you see," she said, "we're going to let you down to the hillside."

Thomas eyed the basket with misgivings. "I'm a big man, Marotta", he said. "Do you think that basket . . . ?"

Fellow had removed the books from Thomas' table. He carried the table across and set it under the window. He turned back with a shout. "Do you think, Master Thomas, that we would bring a basket that wouldn't hold you? Into that basket has gone the skill and love of the finest weavers in Italy!"

Thomas smiled at him. He smiled at Marotta. Just then the light of one of the lanterns fell on her face, revealing the tears in her eyes. Suddenly he felt terribly sad. Suddenly he knew that he was going to miss his donjon tower prison. He was going to miss the morning chats with Marotta, the long and uninterrupted hours of reading, the deep and wondrous stillness of the place.

"Before you go, Thomas," Marotta whispered, "I have things to tell you. I believe they will make you happy."

"What are they, little sister?"

"Do you know the old saying 'Sometimes a conquered man conquers his conquerors'?"

"I have heard the expression."

"Well—you have been the prisoner here, Thomas, but you have captured your jailers."

Thomas chuckled. "I have captured no one."

"You have captured the minds of some of us. Me, for one. I had been thinking about this for a long time, Thomas, but it was only from talking to you—and watching you—that I got the strength to make my decision. I'm leaving the castle tomorrow. I am joining an abbey of the Benedictine nuns."

Thomas held his sister at arm's length, studying her face. "Are you sure?" he asked softly. "Are you sure the religious life is for you? Marriage, too, is a noble vocation."

Marotta nodded. "I am sure. And Landulph, Thomas—you have captured his mind as well!"

"Landulph!" Thomas stared at Marotta in amazement. "Don't tell me that wonderful, overgrown rascal is joining an order!"

"No, Thomas. But he has left the service of the emperor. He is fighting now with an army friendly to the Holy Father."

"I'm glad, Marotta. I'm sure, however, I had nothing to do with it."

"But you did. Landulph told me so. He said it was your courage that gave him courage."

Meanwhile, Fellow and his brothers had made everything ready. One of them stood out in the hall, all set to guide the heavy rope around the tower pillar. The basket stood on the table under the window. The end of the rope was securely looped around it.

"Into it now, Master Thomas!" Fellow shouted. He and one of his brothers helped Thomas to climb up and in. "Now, Master Thomas," he said, "we are going to lift you out of here. When you first feel yourself in midair it will be a little scary, so take my advice. Close your eyes and relax. My brothers and I will take care of the rest."

Thomas smiled. "God bless you, Fellow", he said. "God bless you all. I won't be afraid. There's only one thing." His eyes lifted toward the ceiling.

"What is that, Master Thomas?"

"The watchman on the tower platform. What if he looks over the side and sees me?"

"He'll look over, Master Thomas, but he won't see you."

"Why not?"

"I told you I had another brother, Master Thomas. He is taking the tower watch tonight! Now, out with you!"

It was as Fellow had predicted. When Thomas first realized that he was hanging over dark space with only the basket below and the rope above, he was scared. But he did as Fellow suggested. He closed his eyes. He tried to relax. He said his prayers.

Then slowly, slowly, he felt himself sinking. The wind roared around his ears and swayed the basket. But the three strong men in the tower knew how to guide the rope. Only once did the basket strike lightly against the castle walls. Then it was sinking smoothly, very smoothly, once again. And then, after a long while, Thomas felt a bump below and realized that he had reached firm ground.

He opened his eyes and stood up. White-clad figures appeared out of the shadows and came running toward him. It seemed to Thomas at first that he was being grabbed and helped out of the basket by a dozen arms. Actually there were only two pairs. They belonged to two of his Dominican brothers—to his one-time traveling companion, Brother Robert, and to his revered friend and teacher, Brother John of Saint Julian.

10

THE GREATEST OF CENTURIES

WITHIN DAYS after his escape from the donjon tower, Thomas was a professed Dominican friar. His superiors permitted him to take his vows at once. This ceremony took place in Naples. Some time later, Thomas went to Cologne, the greatest German city of that time, to continue his studies.

It was a golden age. All over Europe there was a growing interest in art and in education. This is one of the reasons why, in later times, the thirteenth century—the century of Thomas Aquinas—would be called the greatest of centuries. Science—"modern science", as it would later be known—was getting under way. Most of the great cathedrals were being built. There were schools everywhere, and with the opening of the century a new kind of school was born—the kind of school future generations would call a university. By the time Thomas reached Cologne in 1248, a larger percentage of the young men of Europe, poor youths and rich ones alike, were receiving a college education than would ever be the case again.

Thomas lived and studied in Holy Cross Convent. His days were full and orderly. He rose at dawn to chant a portion of the Divine Office with his fellow friars in the chapel, attended Mass, and spent the day attending classes, studying, and praying. For four years Thomas stayed in Cologne. There, in 1250, he was ordained, becoming Father Thomas.

One morning after his light breakfast, Father Thomas was studying in his cell before classes began. Sitting at his desk, concentrating on the books before him, he did not hear the light tap on his cell door. The tap came a second time, and a third. Then the door was pushed open. A tonsured head appeared. The head and beaming face below it belonged to a tall Dominican living in the cell next door. Thomas had seen the young man many times;

they had chatted on occasion. He knew little about him, however—only that his name was Peter and that he was popular with his classmates.

Peter coughed to get Thomas' attention. He had a jovial manner and a loud voice. "What a pity to disturb you, Thomas," he shouted, "but I would like a few words with you."

"Come in, Peter, come in. Always glad to talk to you. That is, if there's time." Thomas' eyes went to the small window of his cell.

Peter nodded. "I know", he said. "It's almost time for Father Albert's class. Suppose we walk to the lecture room together. We can chat on the way."

They walked down a long hall and into a sunlit court-yard. Peter began talking at once. "Thomas," he said, "I don't know whether you've noticed this or not. I've had an eye on you for some months."

Thomas' eyebrows lifted slightly. "How kind of you, Peter. How kind of you to take an interest."

" 'Interest' is the word. I am interested in you, Thomas. Do you want to know why? Because you're a Dominican. I think that we Dominicans have got to stick together. We have many enemies at this university, people who say mean things about us. Maybe you didn't know that."

Thomas had to smile. Some members of his own family, he recalled, had said very "mean things" about his order. "I know", he said. "I know we have critics."

"Many critics!" Peter roared the words. "Many!" he

repeated. "As I see it, Thomas, we Dominicans have got to show our critics that we're just as smart as anyone."

"Just as smart?"

"That's right. Just as smart. Take this class we're going to. Father Albert is a Dominican, but he's a very popular lecturer. Lots of non-Dominicans come to hear him. Now Father Albert often gives us a problem to discuss in class. I always get to my feet and take part in the class discussion. Maybe you've noticed that."

"Oh, yes." Thomas spoke rather dryly. "I've noticed."

"But you don't take part in the discussion." Peter thundered at him. "You just sit there most of the time. You say nothing at all. Thomas, do you see what I'm getting at?"

Thomas nodded. He knew what Peter was thinking. Thomas had never been talkative, and the long months in the donjon tower had only strengthened his love of silence and contemplation. He was aware that many students, seeing him so quiet, thought that he was stupid.

He could feel Peter's cow-like eyes fixed hard on his face. "I'm glad you understand", Peter was saying. "I think you ought to take part in the discussions, Thomas. I think you owe it to your order to do so."

"Suppose I have nothing to *say*?"

"Say it anyhow!" Peter guffawed. They had left the courtyard and were in the school section of the convent. Peter's laugh rang loudly through the corridor, so loudly that passing students stopped in their tracks and stared.

Peter ignored them. "Say it anyhow!" He echoed himself and laughed again. "Look here!" He threw a heavy arm around Thomas' shoulder. "Are you having a little trouble with your lessons?"

Thomas hardly knew how to answer. He had never looked on studying as easy. On the other hand, he had never read a book, however difficult, that he had not promptly understood. He replied as honestly as he could. "I study hard", he said.

"I knew it!" Peter's voice was a blast of sympathy. He tightened his hold on Thomas' shoulder. "My friend, will you do something as a favor to me?"

"I'll try."

"The next time Father Albert hands out a problem you can't understand, give me a wink. I'll be at your side at once. I'll explain the problem to you. Then you can take part in the class discussions."

Thomas wanted to laugh; but laughter, he knew, would hurt his tall companion's feelings. He did his best to keep his voice sober. "Of course, Peter. If Father Albert ever gives us a problem I can't understand, I'll call on you for help."

"Three cheers!" Peter withdrew his arm. His eyes were once again fixed on Thomas' face. "I'll tell you why I bring this matter up." He lowered his voice somewhat. "Only yesterday I heard some of the students talking about you. They called you an ox. Was I angry! I said to myself, 'That's an insulting thing to say about a Dominican friar!'"

Thomas glanced down at his ample figure. "Calling me an ox", he said with a smile, "isn't an insult. It's a statement of fact."

Peter's eyes popped open. "Say now!" he exclaimed. "Why don't you speak out like that in class? That's the brightest thing I've ever heard you say." He dropped his voice again. "To be honest, they didn't stop at calling you an ox. They called you a dumb ox." He cleared his throat nervously. "Don't be offended at my telling you this. I mean well."

Thomas was still smiling. "I know you do, Peter."

They had reached the lecture room door. In the crowd of students pushing in, Thomas lost his companion. He made his way through the noisy throng and took the only remaining seat in the rear row.

The lecture room was always crowded when Father Albert talked. Within five minutes students were standing under the tall windows and in the open space behind Thomas. He noticed Peter standing nearby, talking loudly to the men around him. When their eyes met, Peter closed one of his in a wink. He flashed a knowing grin when Thomas winked back.

There was a sudden hush as Father Albert entered and went to the desk on the platform at the front of the big room. Father Albert belonged to a noble German family. He had a commanding manner that made Thomas think of his mother. There, however, Albert's resemblance to any other human being ended. He was unique.

He was perhaps forty years old—he himself did not

know the exact year of his birth. He had the spare frame and wrinkled face of a far older man.

Only his gray eyes were young, terribly young and piercing. He lectured in a thin, tart voice. But he was so wise, so learned, that even the minds of the dullest students caught fire as he talked.

He was famous as a theologian and as a scientist. All over Europe many people spoke of him as Albertus Magnus, meaning Albert the Great. He had devoted years to studying flowers and animals, and had recorded his observations in a series of books. A trained chemist, he was the first man to produce an important medicine—the poison called arsenic—in a free form.

His lecture this morning was on the subject of logic—on the subject, that is, of how to think. He talked steadily for two hours; and for two hours the young men, jamming the room, listened in fascinated silence.

When he had finished, he stood for a silent minute or two, tugging at the folds of his white habit. "All right, gentlemen," he said after a while, "I'll see you again tomorrow. Before leaving I am going to give you a problem. After all, this is a course in logic, so I am going to make a silly statement, an illogical statement. Think it over. Tomorrow I want you to tell me why it's silly. I want you to tell me why the thinking behind my statement is wrong."

Father Albert placed his hands on the desk and leaned toward the students. "This is the statement." He mouthed it slowly and distinctly. "I am a human being", he said. "I

am a person who speaks in a high-pitched voice. Therefore, a human being is a person who speaks in a high-
pitched voice!"

A ripple of laughter ran through the room. "I don't
blame you for laughing." Albert was chuckling himself.
"That certainly is silly. All right! When I return tomorrow I want you to tell me why it is. Good day to you,
gentlemen."

He was gone in a flash of white. He had no sooner left
the room than practically every student burst into talk.
Not Thomas; Thomas simply stared into space, thinking.

He felt a hand on his shoulder. Peter had joined him.
"Well?" he said, leaning over Thomas' shoulder. "Do
you know the answer to Father Albert's problem?"

"I'm considering it", Thomas replied.

"I'll tell you the answer right now. It's silly to say a
human being is a person with a high-pitched voice because some human beings have low-pitched voices. That's
all there's to it. Now when the discussion period opens
tomorrow, I want to see you on your feet, talking."

Peter moved away. Thomas frowned. Peter, he realized, had missed the point of Father Albert's question.
Peter's thinking was sloppy. Thomas shook his head,
distressed. Thomas hated and feared sloppy thinking.
Such thinking, he was convinced, did a great deal of
harm in the world.

He found himself on his feet suddenly, brushing past
the other young men in his row. Peter had stopped in the
center aisle to talk to someone. He saw Thomas heading

toward him and met him halfway. "What's wrong, Thomas?" he inquired. "Didn't you understand my answer to the problem?"

"Yes, but I don't think your answer is right."

Peter's face fell. He regarded Thomas with a hurt look. "You don't?" he inquired. "Why not?"

"Because it doesn't explain why Father Albert's thinking is wrong."

"Can you explain why it is?"

"I believe so. Father Albert's statement is silly because it mixes up essentials and accidentals."

"Essentials? Accidentals?" Peter ground the words between his teeth.

Thomas nodded. "Take our habits, for example, yours and mine. Our habits are made of wool. The wool happens to be white in color. Suppose, now, you ask me to define wool. Suppose I answer that wool is a white cloth. What would you do?"

"I'd laugh. Wool can be any color."

"Exactly. The fact that the wool of our habits happens to be white is an accidental thing. You can't define wool by pointing to an accidental thing about it. You've got to point to an essential thing. The only thing essential about wool is that it is a cloth. That's where Father Albert's statement goes wrong. It tries to define a human being by pointing to an accidental thing about him. It should point to something essential."

In his eagerness to put Peter on the path of common sense, Thomas rushed his words. "You and I", he hurried on, "know what a human being is. A human being is defined in the catechism. A human being, according to the catechism, is a creature made in the image and likeness of God and endowed with a soul. In short, a human being is a child of God. That is the only essential thing about him. Everything else is accidental. Whether his voice is high-pitched or low-pitched, that is accidental. The color of his skin, the color of his eyes, where he was born, or how rich his parents are—all those things are merely accidental. The only essential thing about a human being—the only thing that matters—is that he is a child of God!"

Not until he finished speaking did Thomas realize that another hush had fallen over the big room. All the students had gathered in a circle around him, listening and staring.

When he did realize it, he felt his face turn burning red. He saw one of the students' lips moving and heard him mutter, "Who says this friar is a dumb ox?"

"Who indeed!"

The high-pitched voice coming from the front of the room brought every head around. Father Albert had returned. He was standing once more on the platform, holding a piece of parchment in his hand.

"I beg your pardon, gentlemen", he said. "I had to come back, and I happened to overhear your conversation. I, too, have heard it said that Thomas is a dumb ox." Albert was looking directly at Thomas now. "A dumb ox, eh? Gentlemen, I predict that the day will come when the bellowing of this dumb ox will be heard around the world!"

To Thomas' intense embarrassment there was a burst of applause. Some students clapped, some stamped their feet. Father Albert waved his hands in the air to quiet them.

"That will do!" he cried. "Thomas, may I see you in the hall for a minute? I wish to have a word with you."

The priest left the room at once. The students made a path for Thomas. He hurried through with downcast eyes.

Father Albert, waiting outside the door, held up the parchment in his hand as Thomas approached.

"Did you write this essay?" he inquired.

Thomas peered at the handwriting on the parchment. "Yes, Father Albert. I was wondering what had become of it."

"Apparently you mislaid it. One of the other teachers found it on the floor upstairs. It is a fine piece of work."

"Thank you."

"I see from this that you admire some of the thinking of the pagan philosopher Aristotle."

"I do."

Father Albert smiled. "You know, of course, that some of the scholars in the Church are afraid of Aristotle?"

"So I have heard."

"Their fears are understandable", Albert said. "It is only in the last hundred years or so that we have had translations of all of Aristotle's books. Aristotle is a powerful thinker. Some scholars feel that Aristotle's ideas cast doubt on certain points of Christian doctrine. What is your feeling about that?"

"I don't think they do."

"No?"

"No", Thomas repeated. "In fact, I would like some day to try writing a book on that subject."

"A book about Aristotle?"

"Not about him, exactly. I would like to show that some of the present interpretations of Aristotle's ideas are wrong. I would like to show that Aristotle's real ideas are not opposed to Christian doctrine. On the contrary, they support it."

"I hope you write that book some day, Thomas. I, for one, will be happy to read it." Albert handed the parchment over. "Your essay", he said with a smile. "Now I have another matter to take up with you. Our order has asked me to recommend one of my pupils to teach at the University of Paris. Tell me, Thomas, would you like to go?"

Thomas could hardly believe his ears—or find his voice. "It would be such an honor!" he murmured.

"Good. We will get together soon then and make our plans. Good day, Thomas."

Father Albert hurried away. Thomas stared at the stone floor, thunderstruck—so thunderstruck that he scarcely heard the other students pouring from the lecture room behind him. A number of them stopped to offer friendly greetings. He answered them politely—and went on thinking about the wonderful thing that had just happened to him!

Paris was already a big city when Father Thomas arrived there in 1252. It was a city of song and bustle. It had started, centuries before, as a village on an island in the River Seine. Now this island held only the Old City, with the newly completed cathedral of Notre Dame at one end and a smaller church at the other. To the northwest, the limestone towers of a growing business area spread out over the right bank of the river. People spoke of this area as the town. They spoke of the more thinly settled left bank of the river as the university.

Actually the university was everywhere. Thirteenth-century college students did not attend classes in a group of buildings on a campus. The University of Paris had no campus. Classes convened all over the city in the homes of a score of religious orders.

In a short while, Thomas' lecture room was crowded and his lectures as popular as those of Albert. He worked hard; in fact; he worked endlessly. All day he attended to his duties at the university. Far into the night he sat and wrote in his cell. Books poured from his pen—books that in time would come to be thought of as the heart of Catholic philosophy. Eventually he began the great book he had told Albert he wanted to write. He called it the *Summa Theologica*, meaning a "summary of religion".

About that time a fierce argument broke out among the teachers at the University of Paris. A group of secular

priests headed by Father William of Saint-Amour ac-
cused the members of the mendicant orders—the Dominicans and the Franciscans—of teaching things contrary to Christian truth. Word of the argument reached
the ears of the Pope. The Holy Father promptly ordered
the two sides to send spokesmen to his summer residence
in Italy to argue out their dispute before him. There a
brilliant defense of the mendicant orders written by
Father Thomas carried the day. The Pope permitted the
mendicant orders to continue teaching. He ordered Father William of Saint-Amour and his followers to cease
issuing statements against them.

In 1265, Father Thomas was summoned again by the
Holy Father. He was offered the archbishopric of Naples.
This great honor he politely but firmly declined.

Meanwhile, Father Thomas had left Paris and was
teaching in the papal schools in various Italian cities.
Meanwhile, too, he had become very absent-minded,
as scholars sometimes do. His superiors worried about
him. They feared that Father Thomas, in his absent-
mindedness, would do himself harm. So, when Thomas
left Paris in 1259, his superiors sent another Dominican
priest along to be his companion and protector. This
priest was Father Reginald, a kindly, gray-haired old man.

Thomas and Father Reginald became the greatest
of friends. Thomas spoke to Reginald of matters that he
never discussed with anyone else—his mother, for example. Thomas and his companion often talked of the
proud Lady Theodora. Theodora wrote no letters to her

priest-son, but letters from his brothers and sisters kept him acquainted with her comings and goings.

"You amaze me, Thomas", Father Reginald said to him one morning. "In spite of your mother's cruelties to you, I believe you still love her."

"Very much." Thomas' eyes moistened as he spoke. "God has been good to me, Reginald. Never in my life have I known the ugly feeling of hatred."

He smiled sadly. He was thinking of some of the other members of his family. Landulph was dead. Captured by the emperor, he had died a martyr-like death, fighting in the cause of the Holy Father. Marotta, too, had died, after serving for years as the abbess of her Benedictine house.

Father Reginald acted as Thomas' confessor. He also acted as his secretary. Wherever Thomas went, Reginald went. Wherever they happened to be, Reginald reported to his friend's cell after supper to take dictation.

Coming to the cell one evening in 1264, Reginald found his friend pacing back and forth, talking to himself. The notes in Thomas' hand were not on parchment, but on paper, invented apparently in China, centuries before, but only recently introduced into parts of Europe.

Reginald placed his own blank sheets on the desk. He sat down. He dipped his quill pen in ink, laid it on the desk—and waited. He knew better than to interrupt while his friend was deep in thought.

After a while, Thomas ceased pacing and seated himself.

"Now then," Reginald said, picking up his pen, "what book will we be working on this time?"

"No book this evening, Reginald. I have received a request from Pope Urban the Fourth."

"So? What does His Holiness wish you to do?"

"Something that I hope I can do properly. The Holy Father wishes to start a new festival in honor of the Blessed Sacrament. He has asked me to write the Office, the prayers, and hymns."

"And that's what you have been thinking about?" Father Reginald pointed to the notes in Thomas' hand.

Father Thomas smiled. "I have been trying to think through one of the hymns", he said. "I believe I have it pretty well in mind now, if you don't mind writing."

"Not at all."

Father Reginald's pen hung over the paper on the desk. Thomas dictated slowly. An hour passed, another hour. From time to time Thomas asked his friend to read back what he had written. Occasionally he asked him to change a few words here and there. For the most part he dictated steadily. Firmly and steadily he rolled out the closing lines of a hymn that from that day forth would be part of the liturgy of the Feast of Corpus Christi:

> O thou, the wisest, mightiest, best,
> Our present food, our future rest,
> Come, make us each thy chosen guest,
> Co-heirs of thine, and comrades blest
> With saints whose dwelling is with thee.
>> Amen. Alleluia.

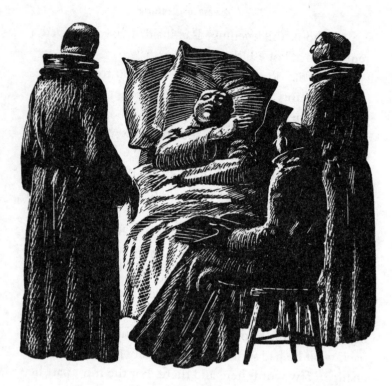

11

THE LAST LESSON

I N THE LITTLE CHAPEL off the church of San Domenico
Maggiore in Naples, Father Thomas was saying
Mass. He was alone in the room save for the old lay
brother who was serving the Mass and three Dominicans, Father Reginald among them. In the morning
stillness the flaring of the candles could be heard. Now

and then the distant murmur of the street made itself heard as people, coming and going in the church beyond, pushed open its front doors.

The lay brother carried the missal to the Gospel side and retired to his proper place. Father Thomas said his prayer at the center of the altar. He made the sign of the cross over the book and read the Gospel for the day. It was December 6, 1273.

Father Thomas finished the Gospel and returned to the center of the altar. He intoned the opening phrases of the Creed and returned to the side of the altar. His voice came out clear and strong. Then suddenly, in the middle of a word, he ceased speaking.

Father Reginald, kneeling on the stone floor behind him, looked up. His good friend had been ill a great deal lately. There was an expression of alarm on Reginald's face. It faded as he saw that Thomas was standing quietly in front of the altar, his eyes on the crucifix above him.

Father Reginald turned his head. The Dominicans with him also looked up. They, too, he could tell, had noticed that Father Thomas was once more in the midst of an ecstasy, that strange experience in which a person, losing for a spell all consciousness of himself, finds his entire attention fastened on God alone.

The ecstasy passed. Thomas picked up the Creed in the middle of the same word, exactly where he had left off. Solemnly the Mass proceeded, the three kneeling monks blending their voices in the responses.

When it was over and Thomas had left the room,

Father Reginald's impulse was to follow at once. A moment's consideration and he decided otherwise. It would be better, he reasoned, to leave Thomas alone for a while with his thoughts. He would wait until evening—until the time came for him to report to his friend's room, as usual, for dictation.

Entering the room, shortly after supper, he found Thomas sitting in a large armchair at one of the open windows. A pale evening sun bathed the cobblestones of the courtyard beyond. The glossy leaves of its single olive tree trembled in a lazy breeze. Thomas had returned to the University of Naples as a teacher three years before. Since then this pleasant room with its broad windows and sturdy furniture had been his home.

He smiled as Reginald hurried, as usual, to the desk, seated himself, and put his writing material in order. He shook his head. "No more work, Reginald", he said.

Father Reginald bent across the table. "Thomas, you know that I was in the chapel this morning. If I am not mistaken, you had another ecstasy." Thomas nodded and Father Reginald continued. "Do you wish to tell me about it?"

"I will tell you what I can." Thomas fell silent and remained silent so long that Reginald began to think he did not intend to go on. He did finally. "Such secrets were revealed to me this morning, Reginald, that all I have written now appears to be of little value." He gestured lightly with one hand, a gesture that took in the desk at which the other priest was sitting. "You understand me, don't you? All my books—they now seem to be so much straw!"

"Thomas!" Reginald sprang to his feet. "You are unwell or you wouldn't make such stupid remarks. I am not surprised. As I was saying to someone only the other day—for twenty years you have worked without ceasing. You have done the work of a hundred men."

Father Reginald went to the sleeping cot at the far end of the room. "Now you are going to get some rest." He pulled back the coverlet. "Lots of rest! I am going to call in the doctor. Something tells me that he will agree with me. When you are well again, we will resume our work."

Thomas was smiling broadly. "Reginald, Reginald!" He shook his large head. "Sometimes you remind me so much of that remarkable woman Lady Theodora."

"Your mother!"

"Mother never listened to a word I said."

"Oh, now, Thomas!" Reginald hurried to his friend. "You know better than that. You know I'm a good listener."

"Most of the time, but not tonight. Did you not hear me say, no more work?"

"But the *Summa*, Thomas!" Reginald moved to the desk. He rested his hand on a clutter of manuscript. "Your *Summa*—the *Summa Theologica*. You have written the first two books of it. You have completed half of the third and last. You must finish that."

"Not I, Reginald. You will have to finish the *Summa*."

"I?" Reginald sank into the desk chair, staring at his friend. "That is a ridiculous thing to say. I don't have the ability."

"God will give it to you." Thomas leaned toward his friend, dropping a hand on his knee. "Believe me, Reginald. I shall never write another word. I can do no more!"

By the way Thomas spoke, the look in his eyes as he withdrew his hand and sat back, Reginald knew that his friend meant what he said. He got up suddenly and turned away. He did not want Thomas to see the tears pouring from his eyes.

A few months before, a message for Father Thomas had arrived from Rome. Pope Gregory the Tenth was planning to bring together the bishops of the Church for a general council in Lyons, France, the following May. He wanted Father Thomas to attend. The bishops would need his advice concerning certain matters of Church doctrine.

Now Thomas took the message from his pocket and held it out toward Reginald. Reginald took it and read it with a frowning face. When he had finished, he turned to the desk, seized a quill pen, and plunged it into some ink. "I will send the Holy Father your respects and inform him that it is quite impossible for you to attempt the journey. You are not well enough to make such a long trip."

"No, no!" Thomas' hand was in the air.

"But, Thomas, you are a sick man!"

"True, I am a sick man. But I am still a Dominican. A Dominican obeys his superiors. Tell the Holy Father that I—you and I—will be in Lyons on May the first, in accordance with his instructions."

Further protests from Father Reginald fell on deaf ears. Owing to Thomas' frail health and to the length of the trip, the two priests left Naples early in January of 1274. They traveled in their customary manner, on foot. They traveled slowly, sleeping at night in monasteries along the way.

A few weeks later they found themselves approaching the coastal village of Terracina, sixty miles north of Naples. It was a windy, sun-drenched morning. Thomas was tired but in good spirits.

"Keep your eyes open for a castle", he told Reginald. "A niece of mine has her home near Terracina."

It was mid-afternoon when Father Reginald sighted the castle battlements, dark against the bright sky. A few minutes later, without a word—without so much as a sigh—Thomas stumbled and fell headlong to the earth.

Reginald hurried to him, turned him over, and murmured a fervent "Thank God!" as he saw that Thomas still breathed. It took all of his own waning strength to pull the large man off the road and into the tall grass. He wrapped Thomas' black mantle around him and placed his own under his head as a pillow. Then, moving as fast as his old legs would allow, Reginald hurried off in the direction of the castle.

He was back in an hour, bringing Thomas' niece and

a body of mounted varlets with a litter. Thomas was taken to the castle and placed in one of its large bedrooms under the care of a hastily summoned physician.

The castle windows were dark when at last he came to his senses. Opening his eyes slowly, he was aware of two men standing by his bed. One of them was Father Reginald. The stranger behind him was a tall man, lean as a lathe. He wore the white habit of a Cistercian monk.

"Thomas!" Father Reginald leaned anxiously over the bed. "Are you awake now?"

Thomas nodded. Reginald's face, he could see, showed the strain of the last several hours. He himself was conscious of a terrible weakness but, at the same time, strangely enough, of a feeling of well-being. "Yes, Reginald," he said, "I am awake."

"Good. Now listen to me, Thomas, and please do not argue. A doctor has been with you. He says that you must not attempt to go on to Lyons. He says . . ."

Thomas interrupted his friend. "I know, Reginald, I have come to the end of my journey." He looked questioningly at the stranger.

"Oh!" Reginald drew the tall monk closer to the bed. "This is the abbot of the Cistercian monastery at Fossa Nuova. He came to us the minute word spread that you were here."

Thomas raised a hand which the Cistercian abbot took, murmuring, "Such a privilege to meet you, Father Thomas, such a great, great privilege." He went on hurriedly. "Our humble monastery is only a few miles away. We would consider it a great honor if you would come to us and let us take care of you."

"And I", Thomas replied with a smile, "would consider it a great honor to be with you."

"But, Thomas!" Father Reginald's voice was shrill. "The doctor says you are not to move so much as one inch from this bed."

"Reginald, Reginald! If the Lord wishes to take me away, it is better that I be found in a religious house than in the dwelling of a lay person."

He was moved that night. Father Reginald argued and objected right up to the last minute, but Thomas' only response was a shake of the head and a gentle "Reginald, Reginald!" As he was borne through the portal of the monastery at Fossa Nuova and past a candle-lit crucifix, he lifted himself slightly from the litter. One of the psalms he loved was on his lips: "This is my resting place for ever; here I will dwell, for I have desired it" (Ps 132:14).

He then lay back and fell into a sound sleep. When he next awakened he found himself in a large cell. Long shafts of sunlight, falling through the leaded panes of three windows, lay across the clean stone floor. Father Abbot had just entered the room. Carrying a load of firewood in his arms, he went to the hearth and knelt before it.

"Father Abbot," Thomas said quietly, "who am I that the servants of God should serve me?"

Father Abbot placed some logs on the fire before making his reply.

"Father Thomas," he said, coming to the bed, "if I were ill, would you not do the same for me?"

"With pleasure."

"Then let me have my pleasure, please." Father Abbot's large eyes looked about the room. "We wish to make you comfortable. Is there anything else I can bring you?"

"Have you a library here?"

"We have. What book do you wish?"

"The biblical book—King Solomon's Song of Songs, the one that is sometimes called the Canticle of Canticles."

Father Abbot left the room at once. He returned shortly, bringing a scroll of the Song of Songs. "This is a favorite of yours?" he inquired.

"A great favorite."

"Then perhaps you will do something for me."

"I will try."

"Let me bring a few of the monks here this evening. One of them will read the Song of Songs aloud, and perhaps you will be good enough to discuss it with them."

Thomas nodded. Shortly after the supper hour that evening, Father Abbot returned, bringing Father Reginald and three of the Cistercian monks. One of the monks read the Song of Songs. He paused after each verse and, for a few minutes, Thomas discussed its underlying meaning.

When the lesson was over, Father Abbot approached the bed. "Father Thomas," he said, "could I bring three other monks tomorrow evening? Could we have another lesson then?"

"Tomorrow evening," was Thomas' reply, "and any evening."

Three different monks came for the next night's lesson and three others for the next. After that it became the custom, shortly after supper, for all the members of the community to come quietly into the room. One of them read the Song of Songs, and Father Thomas discussed it.

Then one evening, in the middle of a discussion, Thomas fell back on his pillow—and was silent.

It was a moment that everyone in the room had long expected. At a nod from Father Abbot, all the other Cistercians left and filed in silence to the monastery chapel. Father Reginald left the room too. He returned in a few minutes, bearing the sacred Viaticum.

Thomas smiled as he saw his old friend making preparations for the last rites. He asked to be sat up so that he might pronounce his final act of faith. His voice was quite firm. His eyes were on the ciborium as he spoke.

"If in this world", he said, "there be any knowledge of this Sacrament stronger than faith, I wish now to use it in affirming that I firmly believe and know as certain that Jesus Christ, true God and true Man, Son of God and Son of the Virgin Mary, is in this Sacrament. I receive thee, the price of my redemption, for whose love I have watched, studied, and labored. Thee have I preached; thee have I taught. Never have I said anything against thee. If anything was not well said, that is to be attributed to my ignorance. Neither do I wish to be obstinate in my opinions, but if I have written anything erroneous concerning this Sacrament or other matters, I submit all to the judgment and correction of the Holy Catholic Church, in whose obedience I now pass from this life."

Thomas Aquinas had spoken his last words. It was early in the morning of March 7, 1274, and, when Thomas died, Father Abbot was the first to speak. "The light of the Church has gone out", he said. "He was a saint."

Father Reginald, finding his own voice at last, corrected him. "Not *was*", he said. "*Is*."

Authors' Note

The writing of any biography of Saint Thomas Aquinas presents considerable difficulty. Saint Thomas' youth reveals few details, the first decade of his life as a Dominican has never been completely and accurately accounted for, and even his final twenty-odd years of life also involve contradictions.

Accordingly, what data are contained in this study have been culled from *Saint Thomas Aquinas* by Father Angelus Walz, O.P., translated by Father Sebastian Bullough, O.P. (perhaps the definitive biography of Saint Thomas), *The Man from Rocca Sicca,* by Reginald M. Coffey, O.P., *St. Thomas Aquinas,* by G. K. Chesterton, and Volume XIV of the *Catholic Encyclopedia.*

This biography, then, contains a fusion of facts with a selection of quasi-facts to render the fictionalized treatment consistent and logical. We have not tried to tell of Saint Thomas' preaching and teaching; we have tried to reveal Saint Thomas himself as preacher and teacher.